Prince
Curse of the

by

Vijaya Schartz

ISBN: 978-1-77145-251-9

PUBLISHED BY:

Books We Love Ltd.
Chestermere, Alberta
Canada

http://bookswelove.com

First Print Edition

Copyright 2014 by Vijaya Schartz

Cover Art Copyright 2014 by Michelle Lee

Dedication

To my mother, who read me fairy tales in the crib, and taught me how to read and write as a toddler, so my childhood would be filled with imaginary wonders. Thank you, Mom. Your strategy worked and enriched my entire life. This story is for you.

Chapter One

Iona Monastery, west coast of Alba - Spring of 806 AD

Friar Gwenvael stared down the rugged cliff and gaped at the giant Drakkars emerging from the morning haze. His heart stampeded to a hard gallop. The garden knife slipped from his hand, and a cold sluice trickled down his spine. *Please, Lord, not again!*

"St. Columba, protect us from these savages," he prayed in a whisper.

With sails furled, the ghostly dragonships glided swiftly toward the fishing village below, like skeletal harbingers of destruction and carnage. Scores of oars, like fish spines, slapped the gray water to the cadence of a muffled drum.

In the air, salty with sea-spray and the smell of fish gut, a spiraling bird cried a warning. Gwenvael pushed back the cowl of his habit to look up. Not a seagull, but a raven... The dark bird dove toward him, a strip of red ribbon trailing from one leg.

As the raven alighted on his shoulder, wings flapping, Gwenvael recognized Ogyr, his sister's pet. "Your warning comes too late, my friend. The Vikings are already here."

The raven cawed then took flight toward the monastery.

"Right." Gwenvael lifted the hem of his woolen robe and raced after the bird toward the cluster of gray stone buildings and thatch-roof huts, half way up the green hillock. His life belonged to the Christian God, but women and children needed protecting. In the desperate race, his bare feet trampled patches of sprouting cabbage, turnips, dandelions and white clover. While barely avoiding the thistles, he could not help but splat his toes into fresh cow dung.

"Viking ships on the shore!" Gwenvael shouted, breathless, upon entering the muddy lanes of the small community. "Hide the relics!"

Friars peeked out of their cottage windows as Gwenvael ran past the dairy and stables. Sheep bleated at the disturbance. Fretful chickens and geese scattered out of his path in a shower of feathers. One fearful monk scrambled toward the chapel.

The bell pealed, alerting the entire monastery. At the sound, Culdee monks rushed out of their huts with wives and children.

When Gwenvael reached the main stone building, he pushed open the cloister door and burst into the vast study full of morning sunlight. A young scholar, the front half of his skull shaved from ear to ear in Culdee fashion, like all the friars, looked up from the intricate illustration on his pulpit, quill poised, with a disapproving scowl.

"The Vikings are back!" Gwenvael panted.

The grating of quills on parchment ceased.

A grizzled friar rolled an illuminated parchment in haste, spilling an ink horn. The gray-hooded monks, young and old, pale with fright, quickly gathered the unfinished pages of St. John's Gospel and scurried out of the study, jostling Gwenvael in their escape.

Dashing back outside, Gwenvael ran along thatched huts towards another stone building. "Vikings on the shore!"

Goats bolted and pilgrims ran, clutching their meager bundles. A woman dragged children by the hand toward the woods while another scooped a crying toddler and sheltered him in the deep fold of her mantle.

A few brave Culdee monks gathered in the courtyard. One brandished a wooden cudgel, another held a spear, remnants of their warring days. Gwenvael kept running, spreading the dreadful news on the morning breeze, like an ominous chant. "The Vikings are back!"

Past the holy thorn streaming with votive ribbons, Gwenvael entered the empty refectory on his way to the abbot's chambers. As he ran past the open windows, he caught a glimpse of dark smoke rising from the burning village two miles down the road. The pillaging had started.

Gwenvael had only heard stories of the last Viking raid on the monastery, thirteen years ago. They'd massacred hundreds that day. How dare the Vikings strike again at the heart of Christendom, and on St. Padarn's day, just after the spring planting?

St. Columba himself had founded the monastery. Had they no respect for the great Saint? Gwenvael reached the abbot's chambers and rushed in without knocking. Inside, the abbot, tall and thin, struggled with a large chest of dark, polished wood.

"Help me!" The abbot motioned to the other end of the chest. "Push. We must save the treasure. Last time they plundered everything. But not today. I will not let them!"

Gwenvael shouldered one end of the chest while the abbot pulled the handle at the other end. "Are these St. Columba's holy relics?"

"Not the relics, simpleton." The abbot grimaced condescendingly. The straight gray hair on his back moved with each shove. "The treasures of the Church."

"The chalice and the silver crosses?" Judging by the weight, there must be many.

The abbot scowled. "The stipends from our benefactors, guilt money for the redemption of mortal sins, the silver and the gold, Friar Gwenvael."

The abbot must have collected much silver, indeed. The two of them could not have lifted the heavy chest. They pushed and dragged it on the flagstone, through the doorway, and across the deserted courtyard, then into the chapel. There, kneeling friars chanted the Pater Noster with trembling voices, as if to draw courage in the face of imminent slaughter.

Three monks broke the ranks to help carry the coffer to the altar where more friars, under the abbot's directions, grappled with the altar stone. The slab moved aside. Inside the altar sat a box the size of a small keg, wrapped in a richly embroidered cloth.

A corner of the fabric fell, and Gwenvael glimpsed a gilded ivory vessel carved in the shape of a toy house. The Monimusk reliquary. Closed with a heavy lock, it contained the very remains of St. Columba. Gwenvael crossed himself.

The abbot fished out the reliquary and dropped it without ceremony into Gwenvael's outstretched arms. The holy bones weighed little. Bemused, Gwenvael watched the Culdee monks struggle to lift the heavy treasure chest and drop it inside the hollow altar. Then they replaced the altar stone and stood the wooden crucifix on top of it.

"Make haste," the abbot yelled at Gwenvael. "Bury the relics under the holy thorn!"

"Amen." Gwenvael re-wrapped the gilded box and carried it outside. He grabbed an abandoned shovel and dug a hole under the gnarled hawthorn tree, beribboned with the prayers of countless pilgrims.

Faint war cries, women's screams, and the stench of smoke floated on the wind and blended with the monotone chant of the Culdees. Gwenvael recited the Pater Noster as he dug deeper. After burying the reliquary, he stomped the dirt then heaped up white stones on top. The cairn would mark the burial place of the holy bones.

With a cry from above, Ogyr the raven dove and landed on the cairn. When the frenzied bird shrieked a warning, Gwenvael listened. A roar of warrior voices rose on the wind, accompanied by the stomping of hundreds of feet.

Glimpsing a flash of sunlight on a swarm of metal helmets, raised spears and battle axes coming up the hill, Gwenvael did not dally, even for a short prayer. While some straggling monks ran for the woods, he rushed back inside the chapel. With the help of two other friars, he barred the heavy door with the iron-clad beam. Then he faced the altar and knelt on the cold flagstone.

Gwenvael joined the chanting, convulsively clasping his hands in supplication. Glancing up, he glimpsed the raven, perched on the highest windowsill.

Muffled sounds of carnage filtered in, intruding on the Lord's Prayer. Outside, warriors yelled in a foreign tongue and people screamed, begging for mercy. The bell toll slowed then stopped. The monks' chant grew hesitant.

When a rhythmic ram thundered against the seasoned oak door, the prayer stopped altogether. Gwenvael drew the sign of the cross as he dared peek at the door. It heaved and bulged under the repeated onslaught.

The crossbar bounced up and clattered to the flagstone. Then the oak panels splintered and crashed inward, trampled by the fur-bundled feet and legs of tall demons with flaxen hair and demented faces. Madness roamed in their pale blue eyes. Wielding long swords, hammers, and battle axes dripping crimson, they stank of blood, sweat, and mead.

Merciful God, please forgive their desecration! From his kneeling position, Gwenvael bowed in submission. This was no time to be foolishly brave. Surely they would spare an innocent friar. *All they want is the silver and gold...*

But the barbarians hacked at the Culdees. A head rolled at Gwenvael's knees, and he recognized the old monk who had spilled the ink horn earlier. He recommended the gentle soul to the Christian God.

Would they all die here today? If God willed it, Gwenvael would accept his fate. Tears rolled down his cheeks as he prayed for a swift end. He had barely reached adulthood. When he saw the shadow of the axe poised over his head, he closed his eyes in surrender.

A yell from the direction of the altar stayed the barbarian's hand. Seconds passed and Gwenvael still lived, as attested by the pounding of his heart. He opened his eyes. The Vikings grumbled and turned to their leader.

In front of the altar stood a big bearded man, bare arms tanned by years of seafaring. A ghastly white scar ran along his left cheek and a leather patch covered the damaged eye. His natural authority marked him as a warlord. He laid his round wooden shield against the altar and spoke loudly in a foreign language. Slicing the air with his axe, the Viking motioned to one of his men who produced a dark haired youth in Viking clothing.

The warlord spoke, facing the monks. Spittle sprinkled his blond beard and moustache. When he paused, the dark youth standing at his side translated the foreign words into familiar Gaelic. Probably a Briton slave...

"I am Prince Bodvar," the Viking explained through the meek voice of the interpreter. "Give me your gold, your slaves, your women, your livestock, and you may live to serve me. Try to hide anything from me, and I'll hack off your head."

The prince's single bloodshot eye surveyed the frightened monks with unmasked contempt. Having spoken, Bodvar sat on the altar in an obvious show of false nonchalance, swinging the bloody axe to and fro like a pendulum.

The abbot rose from his kneeling position and glared at the barbarian. "You have no right in the residence of God! This is a sanctuary!"

Fixing his one-eyed gaze on the abbot, the warlord flashed a half smile while the youth translated, then he pointed to the abbot with his wicked blade.

Two sturdy Vikings grabbed the abbot and brought him before their prince then stepped back.

The abbot's slight frame remained as rigid as his icy green eyes.

Gwenvael held his breath.

Prince Bodvar rose, his helmet towering above the abbot.

"Where is the treasure?" the youth translated.

The abbot kept silent and Gwenvael glimpsed disdain in his thin lips.

For the love of God, Lord Abbot, speak!

The axe rose and fell with a thud. The abbot's headless body wavered before collapsing to the flagstone in a spray of steamy blood. The chapel fell silent, thick with the fear of the quivering monks.

"I will slay as many as it takes," the youth translated.

The one-eyed devil singled out another monk. The friar refused to speak and suffered the same fate. After the fifth execution, Bodvar's demented blue eye set on Gwenvael, who frantically prayed for guidance. *Are riches more important than life, or would the Lord want me to live to praise his glory?*

From its high perch, the raven crooned encouragements.

Confident that the relics would remain safe under the holy tree, Gwenvael obeyed his primal instincts. When the Vikings dragged him before Bodvar, Gwenvael pointed to the altar. "Over there!"

An audible sigh of relief escaped the remaining monks. Gwenvael took pride in the fact that he might have saved their lives, although a few older friars pinned him with glares of disapproval. The Viking prince faced the altar and shoved aside the crucifix, then motioned for his men to heave the altar stone.

With little effort, the heavy slab fell away in a shattering crash that shook the ground and raised a cloud of dust.

The barbarians lifted the chest from the hollow stone forming the altar base then they hacked at the metal lock. The warriors cheered when it broke. Bodvar stepped to the chest and lifted the lid. Flabbergasted, Gwenvael gawked at the sight of such riches. From the chest, the Vikings plucked golden torcs, silver brooches, rings, bejeweled daggers and swords, irreverently donning the priceless things.

Selecting a gold chalice, Bodvar admired it then raised it in a mock toast. "Now," he said with a lurid smile, pointing his axe at yet another monk. "Tell me where the women are."

When the monk lowered his head in silence, the axe rose and fell again. Gwenvael flinched. His blood chilled at the thought of children and women used for pleasure, or slaughtered if they struggled too much.

A cheer outside accompanied the frightened cries of women and children. Gwenvael glanced through the broken door and saw them pushed and dragged across the square. Bodvar laughed and voiced his approval in the foreign tongue.

On his order, the Vikings herded the monks out of the chapel. But when Gwenvael followed them, an axe barred his way. The warrior shoved him away from the door and motioned him toward the Viking leader.

Bodvar grinned with a full row of white teeth. "I make you my personal slave," the warlord told Gwenvael through the interpreter. "You will learn our language, and maybe you can teach me yours." He laughed, as if at a private jest.

Gwenvael nodded to the Viking, unsure whether this personal attention came as a blessing or a curse. From the high windowsill, Ogyr the raven cawed his approval. *Thank you, sister, for your guidance.*

All day, the barbarians looted every dwelling, emptied the cellars, and set the cottages ablaze. That night, they feasted on the monastery pigs, goats and sheep, drank the mass wine and the mead, and raped the women. The Vikings lit great fires inside the chapel, in the courtyard, and down on the beach near their boats. They burned everything, even the abbot's precious furniture.

After hours of drinking and feasting in the warmth of the chapel, Prince Bodvar asked Gwenvael, "Where is the richest monastery worth raiding?"

Gwenvael gasped. It was one thing to sacrifice the treasure to save lives, but quite another to condemn another community to death or slavery. From its high perch, Ogyr cawed as if to catch the young friar's attention.

Gwenvael rubbed his shaven forehead. Although he'd renounced his Pagan gifts, he knew his sister Pressine watched through the raven's eyes. What kind of idea did she try to infuse into his brain? He calmed his mind to listen and suddenly understood. Yes, of course...

Gwenvael smiled for Prince Bodvar. "There is an island, Five days south, where some say legendary treasures are kept. Kingly treasures, magic treasures... I heard of a sword of power that makes a warrior invincible. Some talk about a silver platter, others about a cauldron, a magic spear, and shiploads of gold and silver."

A spark ignited prince Bodvar's blue eye. "How well is the island guarded?"

Gwenvael's heart beat a furious tempo. "My Prince, it is not."

Bodvar lifted a blond eyebrow above the leather patch as the translator relayed the words. The Viking grumbled then tore a piece of meat from a roasted lamb a slave presented on a shield.

"The only guardians of the treasures are women, most of them maidens." Gwenvael prayed he had correctly guessed his sister's suggestion.

The Viking drank from the chalice then burped. "Some women can be fierce warriors."

Bodvar threw a bone at the head of a young, beardless Viking, who ducked it and laughed. With a start, Gwenvael realized the warrior was a woman.

"But the Ladies of the Lost Isle do not bear arms, My Prince." He remembered his brief sojourn among them. "They are young and beautiful, most of them of royal lineage. They study the ancient ways, read and write, seek knowledge, and heal wounds and diseases. They are quite peaceful."

"Writing is evil!" Bodvar frowned as the youth translated. "No men at all?"

"Only a few villagers and aging Druids, My Prince."

"Why are there no warriors?"

"Like this monastery, it is a holy place, My Prince, shrouded in fog even on a clear day." Gwenvael measured his words, careful not to damn his soul with a lie. "But from a distance you can see the circle of stones cresting the cliff, in the shadow of Mount Elenore."

Prince Bodvar bit into another shank of mutton and washed it down with mead. "Tomorrow, we set sail for the island. And you," he pointed the gnawed leg bone at Gwenvael, "will guide us there."

In the glow of the open fire, Prince Bodvar grinned, probably relishing the prospect of easy plunder and beautiful women.

Gwenvael smiled back for a different reason. No one ever reached the Lost Isle unless the Ladies allowed it. Supernatural dangers lurked in the mists surrounding the island. The trespassers never returned, and if anyone could humble the bloodthirsty Vikings, it was the Ladies of the Lost Isle.

* * *

Gwenvael's stomach churned as he stood on the rolling deck of a Drakkar, under a square sail of crimson and white wool. Earlier in the day, four dragonships had sailed north with the loot, livestock, provisions and slaves. Fading in the distance, the smoldering remains of the monastery marked the end of a blessed life steeped in spirituality.

Now, Bodvar's longship led twenty vessels south, toward the Sea of Lyonesse and the Lost Isle. Ogyr the raven circled above the flotilla. Around Gwenvael, battle-scarred warriors twice his size eyed him suspiciously as they stretched gray ropes that moaned against the strain of the wind.

Gwenvael needed to trust his destiny. God threw him to the Vikings to do His work. Must he convert the heathens to Christianity? If so, he must study their language. On the first day, he picked up a few foreign words and decided he could quickly learn the barbarian tongue, which seemed simple compared to his native Gaelic.

The Drakkars sailed for five days, anchoring at dusk to start again at dawn. Only once did the wind drop and the sturdy Vikings had to man the oars to the rhythm of the drums. Njal, the young interpreter, was Bodvar's son from an Irish slave. Njal taught Gwenvael many Viking words. Every so often, Ogyr would fly in reconnaissance then come back to the longship, leading Gwenvael in the right direction.

On the sixth day, the flotilla came upon an island with its base shrouded in fog. Gwenvael thanked the Saints when he recognized the Lost Isle. It had not changed. High above the mist, the forbidding circle of stones stood at the top of a cliff, and above it, Mount Elenore rose, pink with apple blossoms.

"Is this the isle?" Bodvar grinned in anticipation.

"Yes, My Prince, the isle of the maidens." It looked peaceful, but Gwenvael shivered.

Bodvar shouted order, and the Vikings furled the red and white striped sail, stretching the slick ropes. Then the drums beat the tempo, and the oarsmen dipped the oars and started pulling in rhythm.

Gwenvael hid his apprehension behind a strained smile. Although he had renounced the old faith and its magic, he respected the Ladies' might. Now he must brave the wrath of the Goddess along with the barbarians, and hope to survive. He sincerely hoped the Christian God would protect him today.

When the Drakkars entered the fog, Gwenvael felt the rippling of unnatural forces and prayed to his new God as well as to the Goddess. One could never be too sure about the powers stirring the cauldron of human destiny. Even with good intentions, the Ladies of the Isle could prove unpredictable.

As the mist thickened, the longships glided, keeping a safe distance from each other. To avoid collisions, one Viking on each ship blew his horn to signal their presence. The horns kept sounding and answering each other, muffled by the damp veil. The barbarians strained to see through the murk, and so did Gwenvael. Sensing a drop in temperature, he braced himself and tightened his hold on the rigging.

The Vikings also shivered, despite woolen trews, fur vests and furry boots crisscrossed with leather strips up to the knees. Lusty anticipation vanished from the warriors' faces as their eyes grew watchful and wary. Prince Bodvar's helmeted head turned slowly. He reached for the axe at his belt, leaned over the side of the boat and sniffed, as if searching for clues.

"Too quiet," young Njal whispered to Gwenvael. "He hates it."

Gwenvael nodded and swallowed in an attempt to ease the lump in his throat.

The Viking blowing the ram horn stopped and spoke to his warlord. No other horn had echoed the last calls. Frowning, the one-eyed prince ordered the drum to cease. The rowers stopped. Faint cries, and the sounds of a far away struggle pierced the fog, but no other drum pounded. Bodvar's face hardened. When he motioned for the drum to resume, the oars again splashed the water.

Cries of terror at the prow stilled the oarsmen. A rogue wave unsettled the ship and washed over the deck. From the mist, a monstrous dragonhead emerged, loomed, then dove underwater to surface again. The prow of another Drakkar?

Red in the face, Bodvar bellowed orders. Men raced the length of the ship as a sulfurous stench spread.

The sea monster snarled and hissed. It was alive! A powerful tail lashed and sent three Vikings overboard. The black beast shattered the Drakkar's figurehead and pitched the longship at a steep angle.

"Nidhogg!" Bodvar reacted as if he had seen the devil. Brandishing a spear, he aimed and let fly, but the weapon glanced off the slick hide of the sea dragon, which now dove and resurfaced on the opposite flank of the ship.

"Nidhogg! Nidhogg!" The strange word, repeated among the Vikings, spread fear in its wake. In the churning water, floundering warriors yelled for help.

Gwenvael fell to his knees. He now understood how St. Columba must have felt before quelling the sea monster in the Loch Ness. May the Saint forgive Gwenvael for ever doubting the story.

Amidst the creaks and moans of beams, oars broke and the mast cracked but still held. The longship heaved and rolled. The monster roared as it coiled and uncoiled, then rammed the Drakkar, sending men overboard.

Drenched and shivering, Gwenvael seized a rope and pulled himself out of the way. Warriors tumbled or steadying themselves on the row of round shields that lined both sides of the Drakkar. Weapons clattered to the deck. Axes and swords slid to and fro, threatening to slice anything in their path. A wave crashed amidship, drowning the screams of rowers.

The barbarians thrown overboard clamored as they struggled in the gray waters. The snarling monster snatched them with sharp teeth and tossed them, like bundles of hay on a pitchfork, only to catch them in its maws. The beast decapitated one Viking, bit off another's leg, then cleaved a third man in two.

Begging protection from the Christian God, Gwenvael stared, awestruck by the powers the Ladies had unleashed. From his position in the stern, it looked like a battle of will between Bodvar and the beast. They glared at each other, hissing insults and threats, oblivious to the destruction and suffering around them.

With a powerful swat of its tail, the winged serpent breached the hull. Water churned into the ship's bowels as the Drakkar lurched and dipped. The mast splintered, sending whipping ropes and yards of heavy sail crashing across the deck. When the boat tilted, men yelled warnings and screamed in pain, tangled in the rigging of the fast-sinking ship.

The monster rose once again. It hissed then dove, leaving its stink about the wreck. Dropped into the chilly waters, Gwenvael grabbed onto the crippled hull and tugged at one of the great wooden shields. It came free. Heaving himself on the floating shield, he paddled clear of the sinking Drakkar.

Soon, the wreck faded in the thick grayness with the stifled cries of the wounded and the drowning. In the choppy water next to Gwenvael, Prince Bodvar emerged, grappling for a broken oar. He had lost helmet and eye patch, and the long scar that sealed his lost eye showed white on the weathered face.

The Viking sank.

"Eh!"

Shaken by the massacre, Gwenvael could not let another man die. He reached with one hand and pulled up the Viking's head by the hair. "Don't you drown on me. Are you whole?"

Like a mad man touched by the gods, showing no sign that he had heard or understood, Bodvar stared into nothingness.

"Nidhogg!"

Chapter Two

Lost Isle, the same day

Exhausted by the strain of summoning the sea serpent, Pressine collapsed into the cool grass at the top of Mount Elenore. Her head swam as she lay, staring at fast scudding clouds, but she grinned. She had summoned the sea serpent all by herself. Such a stretch of her precious gift, however, had sapped her strength.

Ogyr flew down in a flapping of wings and perched on a small bush nearby.

"You did well, my friend," Pressine crooned.

The bird cawed and tilted its head.

"Thanks to us, the Goddess has destroyed this Viking fleet. It will show aunt Morgane how strong I am." But Pressine could not rejoice yet, not until she knew Gwenvael had survived.

"Pressine!" Morgane called from the Orchard below. She sounded short and irritated. Why?

Pressine pushed herself up despite her dizziness, picked the hem of her blue shift and strolled downhill on wobbly legs. When Ogyr alighted on her shoulder, she stumbled but caught herself. As she wove through the apple trees, pink blossoms snowed on her head, and the breeze carried their fragrance as it blew her long dark tresses.

Pressine stopped in front of Lady Morgane, heart pounding. "Did you see what I just did?"

Morgane scowled. "I see all that happens on this isle."

Like Pressine, Morgane wore the royal blue shift tied at the waist by a golden sash, but the Lady's hair hung in a single braid down her back. She squinted into the bright sun that warmed the land after a long winter. "You should have consulted me. You were reckless to attempt this alone."

"But I did it." Pressine refused to let her aunt spoil her victory.

"Abusing our gift for selfish endeavors carries severe consequences," Morgane snapped.

"I know that." Pressine ignored Ogyr who flew off her shoulder. "I only summoned the Goddess for help. She did the work."

The lady pressed her lips together. "But wasn't your goal to show off your strength? Possibly to impress me?"

Pressine looked down under Morgane's steely stare and sighed. "Perhaps, a little."

"We must not take pride in our special abilities, child."

"I am sorry." Pressine had enough of one curse on her head, she could not afford to anger Aunt Morgane.

"You look tired." The Lady's voice softened. "But you handled the summon flawlessly." The lady almost smiled but not quite. "Next time, let me know before attempting something that dangerous."

"I will." Pressine basked in the recognition. The Lady rarely praised anyone. "I want to make sure Gwenvael is safe."

"I sent rafts to fetch the survivors." The Lady started down the slope. "I wonder whom the Goddess decided to spare."

Vijaya Schartz

Pressine followed at a sedate pace. From this height, she could see most of the island bathed in sunshine, and all around, the magic mist that hung low on the water, like a crown one mile wide. Overhead, Ogyr uttered happy shrieks.

Morgane glanced over her shoulder. "Your reckless enthusiasm may turn against you someday." She sounded concerned. "We need not provoke the Vikings."

"But we won," Pressine crooned, in an attempt to charm her way to forgiveness.

Shaking her head in surrender, Morgane kept walking. "Yes, we did, for now..." When she stopped and turned to wait, her gray eyes softened and she smiled. In that instant, Morgane's ageless face bore a striking resemblance to Pressine's mother.

Pressine cast away the thought. She hated her mother for cursing her.

"You need to learn patience, child." The mild reproach in Morgane's voice stung Pressine.

"You speak like old Merlin." Pressine braced her steps, unwilling to show her fatigue as she caught up with her aunt. "And despite your youthful looks, you think like a crone."

The lady exulted in a clear laugh. "You will, too, in a few centuries. Power comes to us before wisdom, child, but you will learn, in time."

Time... There would be plenty of that.

Morgane grew serious and squeezed Pressine's arm, leading her down the gentle slope. When they reached the circle of stones that crowned the plateau, at the edge of the cliff, the lady sat on a stone bench facing the sea.

24

"The rescue rafts have not returned yet." She patted the space beside her. "Come sit."

Pressine obliged her and dangled her legs as she looked out to sea above the magic fog. Nothing she could do but wait to find out whether or not Gwenvael lived. *Dear Goddess, although my brother is now a Christian, please have mercy on him!*

"Did you think about my proposition?" Morgane's clear voice pierced the breeze.

Pressine frowned at the reminder. Although she understood the necessity to rally the country against the Viking hordes, the sacrifice seemed enormous. "You mean my marriage to that old king?"

Morgane snorted, a strange sound from such a lady. "Thirty-five is not old, child."

The spring breeze made Pressine's blood rush with strange stirrings. "Is the king handsome despite his age?"

"He is brave and wise." Morgane cast her a side glance. "A widower."

"I would have preferred a dashing young man to take my maidenhood." Pressine bent over and plucked a buttercup from the grass, then tucked the flower in the braid crowning her dark tresses. "They say you never forget your first lover."

"Indeed." Morgane gazed faraway to where the sky met the sea. "I will forever remember Achilles."

"See, what I mean?" Pressine crossed her legs like a scribe on the stone bench. "That is the kind of man I want to marry. Not an old king."

"Demigods and heroes make terrible husbands, child, believe me." A faint smile brushed Morgane's lips. "But you should have seen Achilles before the ramparts of Troy, shouting insults to Memnon."

Pressine patiently indulged her aunt as the chirping of sparrows intruded. She hoped that when she reached Morgane's advanced age, she would refrain from recounting the same old stories.

"...what a glorious combat, when he killed the Prince of Ethiopia..." Morgane's gaze searched the azure sky. "Of all the men I loved, Achilles still haunts my dreams."

Pressine's sigh escaped unbidden. "I guess any kind of service to the Goddess must be better than rotting in this secluded place. I miss home. Does the land of Alba resemble my native Bretagne?"

"Elinas of Dumfries rules over the tribal kings and barons of Strathclyde. You will enjoy the lakes, the forests and the bubbling springs." Morgane's expression remained neutral. "The country needs a high king to unify and protect the land."

"I would have preferred a Scot, a Pict, even an Angle." Just mentioning the wild northern tribes filled Pressine with tingling curiosity. "Britons are so tame."

Pressine hated the assignment, but she had sworn to serve the Goddess.

Morgane smiled. "I need a royal virgin to seduce him into marriage, a delicate and vivacious beauty wielding the might of the Goddess. With such a brilliant mind, you are the perfect choice."

How Pressine resented Morgane's manipulative ways.

The Lady smoothed Pressine's dark hair. "What man could resist these lustrous tresses? Or those eyes, clear as a mountain stream in sunlight?"

Pressine pulled her head back. "How do you propose I make him high king over all of Alba?"

"Do not fear." Morgane squeezed her hand. "The Goddess will provide opportunities and give you signs. Will you obey Her will?"

Although her heart grew heavy, Pressine knew she must obey. "Do you think I can learn to love Elinas, in time?"

Brushing a small sprig from her shift, Morgane sighed. "Do you know the hardest part?"

"No." What terrible secret had Morgane kept from her?

"It is sad to see your mortal lover whither and die while you remain young and vibrant." Morgane paused. "And never underestimate the power of the curse."

"Aye, the curse..." The mention of it made Pressine shudder. She now understood its severity and felt the oppressing threat closing upon her. "I wish I could forget Mother's cruelty. She ruined my life."

"Hush, little one." Morgane patted her hand. "Nothing you can do but accept your fate. King Elinas must never see you in childbed."

"But, if by misfortune he does?" Pressine's throat clenched and her voice cracked.

"You will lose each other," Morgane said, matter-of-fact. "The kingdom will wither, the wealth dwindle, and the king's sons be cursed for nine generations." She stared into Pressine's eyes. "So, will you wed the Briton king?"

Pressine straightened her back and forced down her dread. No one would ever accuse her of shirking her duty. If the Goddess requested she marry King Elinas, so be it. She took a deep breath. "When do I leave?"

"Tuesday, of course. Have you learned nothing of our ways? You of all people should know the most auspicious day to start on a journey."

"Tuesday?" It seemed so sudden.

"You have three days." Lady Morgane rose and glanced down to the shore below. "The first raft is emerging from the mist. Let us go meet the survivors."

Still stunned by the news of her impending departure, Pressine surveyed the beach below. Beyond the surf, a raft approached to the slow rhythm of a paddle. The priestess who had guided the rescue boat through the mists stood on the flat deck.

Pressine scanned the sitting figures huddled on the raft. *Dear Goddess, please let it be Gwenvael!* She stood up and hurried down the stairs cut in the face of the cliff, a steep shortcut to the beach below.

Gusts of wind whipped her shift, and sea spray dampened her hair. Behind her, Morgane followed at a lady-like pace. A second raft emerged from the mist as Pressine reached the base of the cliff.

She hurried toward the shore, her booted feet sinking into sand. The boatman leapt into shallow surf and dragged the boat onto the wet sand. The silhouettes on deck slowly unfolded.

Desperate to find out whether or not her brother lived, Pressine searched the shivering refugees.

Although she had prayed, the Goddess offered no guarantees. Magic often worked in unexpected ways. Sometimes, it escaped the bonds of the spell and took a life of its own, crushing everything in a destructive frenzy. And on occasion, Pressine had seen people spared by the sea serpent, only to go mad or die of fright.

"Gwenvael!" She called toward the gathered survivors.

When a young man looked up and waved, she ran to her brother. Relief washed over her. *Thank you dear Goddess for sparing his life.* She hugged him tight and felt his laugh against her chest, then she held him at arm's length.

"I was spared, sister." The Culdee tonsure made Gwenvael look older. Salt water had reddened his eyes in a pale face. He turned and nodded toward another youth, who supported a dripping giant with long flaxen hair. "This is Prince Bodvar and his son Njal."

A horrible scar twitched on the Viking's face, as a single blue eye stared into emptiness. Pressine shuddered. She recognized the warlord from a vision, but the man had changed. He looked as if he had just visited the land of the dead and would forever gaze upon it.

"Nidhogg!" the barbarian blurted in a daze. An empty scabbard dangled on his thigh as he leaned heavily on the youth.

Pressine wondered at the foreign word. It sounded ancient.

Gwenvael motioned toward a dozen shivering men, who gratefully accepted blankets from the maidens come to help. "It seems no other Vikings survived the onslaught, only a few Briton slaves."

Pressine stepped aside when Morgane reached the rafts.

After a quick glance at the survivors, the Lady addressed the priestess who had guided the rescue through the mist. "Warm them, feed them, and let them sleep in the Druids' hall. Don't spare the firewood or the mulled wine. When their color returns, they are free to stay or leave as they choose."

Morgane then pointed at Bodvar. "This man needs help."

The Lady nodded to a couple of fishermen who had stopped mending their nets to assist with the refugees. "Bring him to my cottage. Pressine, come with me."

Pressine nodded, curious about the Lady's intentions.

After the men relieved Njal of his burden, the youth wrapped himself in a blanket. Gwenvael waved at Pressine as he headed toward the druids' hall with his young friend and the other survivors.

The two fishermen half carried, half led the confused Viking, and followed Morgane who skirted the base of the cliff along the stream. Pressine walked behind them, wondering what Morgane had in mind. If Bodvar had lost his wits, only the Goddess could help him.

As the strange party crossed the village, geese scattered and honked in a flurry of feathers. Pressine held her breath at the stink of urine surrounding the tanning shed. At the laundering pool, women stopped pounding clothes and stared at the drenched Viking with open curiosity. Between the bath house and the dairy, the small party took the lane that wound its way up a grassy hillock in the direction of the cottages.

The beehive-shaped stone buildings, with narrow holes for chimney and windows, served as individual dwellings for the priestesses. One needed privacy to practice the magic arts. Pressine ducked through the hide covering Morgane's doorway. The small circular room could scarcely hold five people.

Bodvar groaned when the fishermen laid him among the furs on the low pallet. A servant girl brought wool blankets, handed them to Morgane, then rushed out. The fishermen left as another girl carried in steaming bowls of mint brew and broth.

Pressine took the tray from the girl. "Thank you. Now revive the fire and warm some vinegar."

Seemingly unaware of his surroundings, Bodvar whimpered between chattering teeth.

Morgane tugged at the big man's fur vest. "Help me remove his clothes."

Pressine approached the quivering Viking and helped her aunt lift the heavy man's shoulders and pry off his armor plates. Deftly, Pressine loosened the crisscrossed leather straps holding the furry leg coverings. Morgane unlaced the leather jerkin, baring a well muscled chest. After removing the scabbard, belt, and hard leather cod piece, Pressine hesitated.

"Hurry," Morgane pressed as she unfastened the ties at the man's waist, then she pulled down the wet woolen trews, exposing the Viking's powerful body.

Morgane's interested gaze coursed the splendid naked man. "What a waste. Look at him."

How could she not look! Pressine had never seen a naked man before, and she suspected this one to be exceptionally healthy. A violent spasm coursed along Bodvar's body.

Pressine refocused on the task at hand. "Are you going to use magic to revive him?"

Morgane scowled. "You should know better than to ask. Magic is allowed only for the service of the Goddess."

Bodvar muttered incomprehensive foreign words through his trembling.

The serving girl approached the bed with a jar. "The vinegar is hot. And I have brew warming on the hearth."

Morgane took the jar of vinegar. "You can go now."

After the girl left, Morgane motioned to Pressine. "We must rub the hot alcohol into the skin to warm his blood."

Despite their ministrations, the shivering persisted, even after a blazing fire made the two women glisten with sweat. Pressine trickled hot brew between Bodvar's chattering teeth, but the barbarian coughed it up and kept shaking uncontrollably.

Pressine felt his forehead. "Still cold as a frozen brook."

"He needs body warmth." A twinkle danced in Morgane's eyes. She took a sharp breath. "We shall hold him between us, skin against skin."

Nodding, Pressine discarded shift and boots. She kept only her linen chemise, but when Morgane disrobed entirely, Pressine did the same. The Viking's nakedness felt like ice against her round breasts and flat belly.

She tried to ignore the warrior's shriveled maleness. Should she feel excited like Morgane? Pressine did not find the experience arousing at all. Focusing on the shivering body, she willed her heat to infuse the giant's skin and stiff muscles.

Covering themselves with wool blankets, the two women huddled with Bodvar under the covers. It took a while, but the tremors finally abated and some warmth returned to his skin. As Pressine stepped off the pallet and reached for her chemise, the man's eye opened and bulged.

"Nidhogg!" he screamed.

"His mind is gone." Pressine slipped on her chemise and shift. Then she stuffed the bed with warm stones from the hearth. That done, she fed the Viking some more broth. "What's Nidhogg?"

"Dread-biter, the scourge of the Viking gods." Morgane, now in her chemise, stirred a potion in a wooden bowl. It smelled of chamomile with a hint of bitter poppy. "In Norse legends, Nidhogg takes the shape of an evil dragon to devour corpses and gnaw at the root of Yggdrasil, the Tree of Life."

Awed by the extent of Morgane knowledge, Pressine understood. "Then Bodvar thinks the sea-serpent is this Nidhogg dragon?"

"So it seems." Morgane poured the potion into a bowl. "This will help him sleep. Tonight, I shall make him whole again."

Pressine meant to ask how, but Morgane's expression, as she hushed her out the door, barred any further question.

* * *

Bodvar remained in Morgane's cottage for the next two days, and the Lady forbade anyone to come near. What secret magic did she weave around the Viking prince? Not that Pressine wanted to visit. An expedition to woo a king required planning, and she had little time to spare.

The best seamstresses on the isle sewed rich dresses in haste. Skilled stitchers also added gold and silver trim to her finest clothes. More importantly, Pressine supervised the removal of her personal treasures from the secret cave for her royal dowry.

* * *

The night before Pressine's departure, two scores of priestesses, young and old, gathered around the moonlit circle of stones on the top of the cliff to celebrate the full moon and bless Pressine's mission. They invoked the Goddess, circling sunwise, weaving between the monoliths as they chanted the song that binds heaven and earth.

Dressed in a thin white robe, Pressine drank the bitter potion. The air charged with the might of the chant made it difficult to breathe, but she felt ready to be empowered for her sacred endeavor. She approached the central stone slab with confidence then reclined upon it.

Morgane unsheathed a long sword that reflected the moonlight and rested it upon Pressine. In the chilly night, pinned between the cold rock at her back and the naked blade flat on the length of her body, Pressine stared at the stars. Her cold fingers enfolded the hilt that formed a cross between her breasts.

When the chanting ended, Morgane faced the low altar where Pressine lay. The Lady raised both hands towards the moon.

"O Mother Goddess, Mistress of light and darkness, empower your maiden, and the sword Caliburn forged in the otherworld by Gofannon, god of smithcraft. Render woman and blade enticing to Elinas, the chosen high king of Alba. Give Pressine strength in the struggle to come, protect her from malevolence, and grant her victory in your name."

A current raced through the sword from point to hilt, warming Pressine's body. She tingled with bursts of warm energy that emitted a blue radiance. In the glowing aura above her, the Goddess appeared as a sea serpent unleashing its fury upon an invisible enemy. When the serpent entered the sword, Caliburn's blade shook with life in Pressine's grip then shone blue before resting, inanimate but warm, on her supine body.

Offering thanks to the Goddess, the priestesses closed the ritual with a chant of gratitude. Flushed by the experience, Pressine rose and returned the blade to its bejeweled scabbard. Then the ladies filed out of the stone circle and down the steps of the cliff, and Pressine carried the empowered sword into her cottage.

On the way there, the smell of roasting meat and freshly baked bread from the feast in the druid's hall reminded Pressine she had nothing to eat all day. After wrapping Caliburn in blue silk, she stored it in a travel chest. Then she hurried to the feast, guided by the heavenly aroma and the sound of laughter.

She stopped on the threshold to search for Gwenvael. Around the central fire illuminating the high-vaulted building, druids and ladies sat in a wide circle on the rushes covering the flagstone. Among them, the survivors of the battle looked fully recovered.

Morgane did not preside at the feast, neither did the Viking, and Pressine wondered at their absence.

With a pang of regret, Pressine realized it would be her last celebration in the Lost Isle. She spotted her brother and his new friend, Njal. As she joined them and sat cross-legged, they welcomed her in their midst. On thick bread trenchers, the cooks served roasted lamb with dandelion greens, then hot cakes. The goat cheese on fresh bread with salted butter tasted wonderful.

Pressine ate and drank the sweet fermented juice of apples and reminisced with Gwenvael about their childhood. Late into the night they laughed and sang. Older folks retired while scattered revelers still conversed in low tones. At the edge of the glow from the fire, isolated silhouettes retreated to the corners of the hall and spread their blankets to sleep.

After Njal took his leave, Gwenvael scooted closer to Pressine. He looked fearful. His foreskull, freshly shaved from ear to ear, gleamed in the orange glow of the flames.

His brow furrowed. "Are you taking your dowry with you?"

"Yes." Pressine smiled. "What royal bride would not come with plenty of gold and silver? I will also carry special gifts from the Lady."

Gwenvael shook his head. "'Tis dangerous to travel with such a fortune. Without a war band, I mean... I had an armed escort when I brought it here."

"Trust me." Pressine laid one hand on her young brother's shoulder to reassure him. "The Goddess protects Her own."

"I hope she does." Gwenvael tightened the blanket around his shoulders. "Lucky our royal father provided for you."

Pressine smiled at his innocence. "Luck had naught to do with it. We make our own destiny."

A log collapsed in the fire, sending incandescent sparks to the high ceiling, and beyond through the smoke hole.

Gwenvael glanced up. "Mother often asked about you."

"Never mention her in front of me." Pressine regretted her sharp tone, but she shook inside at the very thought of her mother's cruelty.

Gwenvael shook his head in a way that reminded Pressine of the little boy he had been. "I admire your independence, sister. It takes courage to follow the Goddess."

"I have no other choice." Pressine stared into the embers, realizing she would never be free to choose her destiny. She swallowed the knot in her throat. "But things are as they should be." She glanced up and smiled. "What of our beloved Bretagne?"

A boy servant threw a new log on the ebbing fire, eliciting a shower of crackling ambers. New flames rose and hissed.

Gwenvael spat into the fire as if to ward off evil. "Just when we change the name of Armorica to Bretagne to fit us Britons, our father king sells our country to the Franks. It sickens me. Armorica was wild and free. What good is a country called Bretagne, if it pays tribute to the Franks?"

"It's all because of the Christian shrew who stole our mother's king." Pressine could not help the scorn in her voice. "At least, she will never bear any pups."

Pressine had made sure of that when she had cursed the princess to remain barren. But Pressine had paid dearly for the vengeful deed. In return, her mother punished her with a curse of her own.

Gwenvael sighed. "Becoming a Christian makes our father a powerful man. King Salomon of Bretagne, Paladin-knight of Charlemagne!"

Drawing a finger to her mouth, Pressine nodded toward the sleeping silhouettes in the shadows then whispered, "Perhaps our father king tried to spare his people unnecessary war, and maybe he was right."

Gwenvael nodded gravely. "Perhaps."

Pressine shivered despite the fire, remembering how, as a child, she had misjudged her father. "But why did Father refuse Merlin's help in times of need?"

"The odds were against him," Gwenvael whispered. "Charlemagne and his bishops believe druids are evil."

"But you are a Christian monk and you do not," Pressine observed flatly. "And Charlemagne himself takes counsel from a seer, the Great Malagigi."

The light of the flames danced on Gwenvael's smile. "Malagigi is an enchanter, not a sorcerer."

"I see no difference." Pressine shrugged. "Just another name for the same purpose."

Gwenvael laid his hand on hers, a reassuring gesture from childhood. "You cannot keep the world from changing, sister. Yesterday the druids, today the Goddess against Charlemagne's bishops, tomorrow, who knows? If we are not careful, we could be worshiping Viking gods."

Pressine stared at her brother in surprise. "What are you saying?"

"I fear the raids over the past few years are only the beginning of a great invasion." Gwenvael glanced up at her, as if wondering how much to tell. "They want all the land."

"How do you know that?" Pressine considered her brother with renewed interest. "You renounced your gifts."

"Njal told me." Gwenvael's soft brown eyes gazed at her in earnest.

Pressine shuddered at the memory of her visions. "I saw them terrorize the people of this land. That is why I agreed to marry King Elinas, to give him a better chance to fight back."

Gwenvael remained quiet for a moment. "I think I found my calling."

"Calling?" the word sounded strange to Pressine.

"I must convert the Vikings to the gentle ways of our Lord Jesus." Gwenvael looked too young and frail for such a task. "I shall go among them and preach, like St. Columba among the Picts."

Pressine cringed at such a dangerous task, but she understood. At least, the Christians were civilized. Still, she feared for her only brother. "I hope your god protects you well."

"I trust He will." Gwenvael flashed a strained smile.

"Promise me you will be careful." Pressine shivered and tightened the shawl around her shoulders. She had serious misgivings at the threshold of this new life.

* * *

On Tuesday morning, the islanders stood on the shore to bid farewell to Pressine and her retinue. Two large flat boats with sails, ready to carry the party to Alba, bobbed gently just a few white-crested waves away from shore.

Through the shallow water, villagers led stubborn ponies and oxen to the large boats. On the shore, bleating goats, sheep and skittish horses awaited their turn. Servants also loaded barrels of grain and mead for the journey.

Seven boys and seven girls between the ages of ten and twelve, dressed in blue tunics, each with a golden sash, now boarded the boats to escort Pressine on her journey. Ogyr circled overhead. When the raven shrieked, Pressine glanced back.

Morgane walked toward her on the beach with Bodvar, Gwenvael, and the young Njal. To Pressine's surprise, Bodvar held Morgane by the waist in a possessive embrace. He looked fully recovered, coherent, and a new leather patch covered his missing eye. He smiled contentedly.

How did the Lady manage that miracle? Pressine took mental note of this unconventional healing method. Bodvar's tender demeanor and clean attire did not suit him. The fearsome Viking looked like a silly white bear.

Morgane's aura radiated with the afterglow of lovemaking. "Bodvar and Gwenvael will accompany you to your destination before joining the Viking fleet in the northern wilderness."

Concerned, Pressine turned to Gwenvael. "Are you certain you will be safe with him?"

"Quite." Gwenvael beamed. "The Lord answered my prayers. Bodvar wants to make me his blood brother for saving his life. He will take care of me. I hope to make him my first convert."

Glancing at the formidable barbarian, Pressine felt troubled. "Truly? You trust him?"

"He vowed on his honor as prince and warrior." Gwenvael chuckled. "Besides, Njal is staying here with Morgane, as some kind of hostage."

Morgane ruffled the younger boy's hair. "I can educate the little weasel. His mother is a Celtic princess. A prince of mixed blood might come in handy when peaceful alliances are called for." She patted her belly. "I also have another child in reserve, just to be sure."

Pressine rolled her eyes. Morgane carried the Viking's bastard! No wonder she bathed in radiance.

Bodvar nodded as if he understood. His raucous laugh blended with the sound of the surf. He gave Morgane a lusty kiss that made Pressine turn away with embarrassment. How she wished someone kissed her like that.

Gwenvael and Njal clasped arms in farewell.

Then Morgane held Pressine at arm's length. "If you need any help at all, use the water basin or send me Ogyr. In any case, let me know about your progress." She hugged Pressine and whispered against her cheek, "You will never be very far from my thoughts, child."

Pressine would miss the sweet lavender fragrance of Morgane's hair. She struggled not to choke on her words. "Thank you, Aunt Morgane."

"I will keep you in my sight. And if you cannot contact the Goddess on your own, I shall inform you of Her wishes."

Boots in hand, hitching up her skirt, Pressine waded into the foaming surf, followed by Gwenvael and Bodvar. A gust of wind billowed her skirt. She did not glance back, fearing Morgane would see her tears. Once on the flat barge, where her coffers and her retinue waited, Pressine waved to Morgane.

Bodvar and Gwenvael pushed the boat out to sea then climbed on deck. Pressine's vessel passed the second boat to take the lead into the mist. Standing at the prow, Pressine faced the cloudy veil, arms open and eyes closed.

"O mighty Goddess, lead us safely through the mists."

In her mind, Pressine visualized the rocky coast. She heard Ogyr's cries far ahead, but everyone remained silent during the passage through the magic fog. Only the rhythmic grating and splashing of the oars punctuated the raven's calls. Then she felt the warmth of the morning sun on her face. The cheers of sailors and passengers told her they had emerged on the other side of the mist.

Thanking the Goddess, Pressine opened her eyes to behold the scintillating sea. She glanced back to check on the second boat. Reassured, Pressine noticed Bodvar's expression of intense relief. She smiled inwardly. The Viking would not soon forget his encounter with the sea serpent... or the Lady of the Isle.

The rugged coast Pressine had seen so close in her mind, still lay far ahead beyond the horizon. The boats would follow it north to Galloway. When the sailors stilled the oars and unfurled the sails, a strong breeze made the boat lurch forward. The Goddess had blessed them with good wind.

Nausea rose to Pressine's gullet. Was it the swell of the waves, or the sudden realization that she now stood alone in the face of an impossible task? How could she unite the many tribes of Alba against the Viking aggressor? For the first time in her life, Pressine felt small and vulnerable in the face of such a responsibility.

Sensing the prickly drill of an unfriendly stare on her back, Pressine turned for a glimpse of Bodvar, her sworn enemy... The Viking held her gaze then turned away and exchanged barbarian words and sign language with Gwenvael.

What would become of her brother? What awaited Pressine in Alba? Would she even like King Elinas?

Chapter Three

Forest of Strathclyde, two weeks later.

King Elinas usually enjoyed hunting with his retinue, but this morning, the barking dogs and trampling hooves did nothing to lighten his heart. Spring blossoms and aromatic ferns sweetened the breeze in vain. Even the blare of a faraway horn failed to improve his mood. The recent Viking raids on the coast of Galloway weighed upon his mind.

The gray steed snorted and shook its mane, digging its hooves into the muddy ground. Over the squeak of saddles and the chatter of voices, Elinas heard a different sound, soft and melodious, yet powerful. A woman's song?

He halted the horse and raised his hunting spear to command attention.

The conversations stopped. Barons and chieftains in leather gear, as well as ladies in colorful dresses, steadied their mounts. The kennel master restrained a brace of deerhounds straining on the leash.

All Elinas could hear now in the soft breeze, besides the panting dogs and chomping horses, was the rustle of leaves and the shrieks of a raven circling overhead. With a sigh, he dismissed the heavenly voice to the vagaries of his imagination.

He signaled the kennel master. "Let them run!"

Free of the leash, the hounds bounded ahead, noses to the ground, sniffing every tree, and occasionally lifting a leg. Scouts galloped to the front on sturdy ponies. Unhooking his cloak, Elinas called his squire and let the garment fall into the boy's arms.

The first rays of sun warmed his leather jerkin and trews. When a pretty woman gave him a suggestive look, Elinas dismissed her with a wave of the hand. Many ladies fancied themselves as his future queen. Little did they know...

Elinas held up his mount to fall behind the chatty barons and ladies.

"Dewain!" He motioned to his kinsman and counselor to slow his mount and fall into step with the royal steed. "Entertain me with your clever conversation, old friend."

The baron grimaced under his woolen hat, rubbing a leather-clad thigh with wiry fingers as he rode alongside the king. "What a glorious morning for a deer hunt, sire." Dewain begrudged a toothless smile, sending the ends of the red and black ribbons braided into his beard fluttering in the breeze. "Twenty years ago, I might have enjoyed it."

"Come, now, Dewain." Elinas smiled at his friend's antics. "You are still a keen hunter. Will my late father's champion go soft on me?"

Dewain's beady eyes brimmed with intelligence. "No, sire. I still love rounding up game on the royal estates. It reminds me of my youth with your father."

Elinas rubbed an itch that plagued his short-clipped beard. "One of my farmers sighted a white stag in these parts a few days past. 'Tis mating season. The hounds should catch the scent."

"Mating season? Indeed!" Dewain drummed the pommel of his saddle as he rode. "My mating days have long passed, sire, but it is high time to find you a new queen."

Elinas balked at the thought. The old goat had waded into forbidden territory. "I had a queen once, Dewain, and I do have an heir. And if Mattacks should die, I have two more sons to replace him. I do not need a wife!" Elinas spurred his steed and bounded ahead.

Dewain caught up with him. "But sire, you are still in your prime." He glanced sideways at Elinas, as if pondering whether or not to speak his mind. "Your subjects of the old faith believe that a kingdom cannot prosper without a queen. Besides, you need to make alliances."

Elinas cringed but remained silent.

Dewain scowled. "King Alpin MacEochaid, in Dalriada, has many wives, all of them daughters or sisters of defeated kings or potential enemies. Blood alliances last longer than a truce."

"I know." Elinas had heard the argument many times. Imitating Dewain's voice, he said, "And Loth of Lothian, in Dunbar, has many Saxon wives, and even more concubines."

Elinas shrugged then went on seriously. "How they can manage such households, wage war, and still rule a kingdom puzzles the mind."

"Nonetheless, sire, a king needs wives for making dynasties, and concubines for his manly pleasures." Dewain flashed a toothless smile.

Elinas remembered the old man's reputation with the ladies but bit back a sour remark.

"Love and marriage should never mix, sire." Dewain winked. "It has brought down the greatest kings. Remember the stories the bards sing in the halls at Shrovetide? About Arthur, the Bear of Britannia, who made the mistake of marrying for love? It destroyed him in the end."

"Stories, Dewain, only stories." Elinas stiffened in the saddle and surveyed the surrounding woods. "Believe me, one woman was quite enough for me, and with her death, the will to love another has gone forever. I shall not remarry."

Dewain looked suddenly aged. "Sire, for the sake of your kingdom, I beg you to reconsider."

"Nonsense! My kingdom needs a fair ruler, a warrior king to protect it from the Vikings, not a lover of women." Immediately regretting his outburst, Elinas lowered his gaze. In a subdued voice, he said, "The truth be told, I could not bear to see a stranger in my dear queen's chambers."

Dewain glanced sharply at the king but remained quiet.

"I left her rooms intact since the day of her balefire." Elinas looked up ahead to make sure no one rode close enough to hear. "I like to think that she still resides there, just out of sight, singing as she spins her yarn. Sometimes, I can almost hear her sweet voice..." *As I thought I did, just a while ago.*

Dewain sighed. "I understand, sire, but it has been almost a year."

"Do not concern yourself, dear friend." Elinas forced a smile. "Mattacks, my Edling, might make blood alliances in his own time as you suggest, but it is too late for me."

Dewain rolled dark eyes. "I doubt young Mattacks would approve of such practices, sire.

Although his hot blood might welcome the idea, he pays too much heed to the new religion."

Surprised, Elinas turned in the saddle to face his friend. "How so?"

"I hearsay that since fostered at Lord Emrys' castle in Whithorn, the Edling has become a staunch Christian of the most righteous sort." The old jaw tightened under the beribboned beard. "I fear his allegiance to the bishop of St. Ninian and to Charlemagne's Roman pope runs deeper than his Celtic roots."

"Perhaps." Elinas took a deep breath. "Like you, I always favored the old ways, but the young must go with the new, and if the future of Alba resides with the Christian faith, I wish him well. What does it matter which gods rule the heavens? A human king must still rule the land."

"On the other hand, the Christian church is rich and powerful. Mattacks might find it a strong ally." An amused smile played on Dewain's thin old face. "But in the meantime, I do think you would rule more adeptly with a queen at your side."

"You never yield, do you?" Elinas shook his head in frustration.

Dewain gazed deep into the king's eyes. "I know you well, Lord King, and it pains me to see you unhappy."

Elinas broke the stare with a wave of the hand. "I find this conversation tiresome, you stubborn goat."

"It is the privilege of my years, sire." Dewain chuckled. "While most consider me half-witted from old age, I can proclaim the truth and no one takes offense."

"Be gone. Go preach to the barons and leave me be." Elinas smiled to soften the harsh words. "I have important decisions to make, and these familiar woods give my soul some peace in which I can think."

"As you wish, sire. I shall tell the hunters to leave you to your musings." Dewain spurred his mount forth, toward the main hunting party.

Slowing his steed, Elinas let the barons and ladies forge farther ahead. When they had disappeared among the foliage, he glanced back. Seeing no one close, he veered off the trail, in the direction of a chestnut grove he used to roam as a young man. According to the druids, the bubbling spring in that clearing honored Coventina, the River Goddess. The thought of a refreshing draft made him thirsty all of a sudden.

Intoxicated by the temporary freedom from the pressures of his entourage, Elinas bubbled with renewed life force, light and young again. In a copse of oaks, movement caught his attention. Something darted through the underbrush. Sighting the rump of a white hind, the king spurred his steed into a carefree race.

Far from him the idea of killing the splendid beast worthy of a king's spear... Elinas relished the chase for the pure joy of glimpsing the doe's alluring flanks. Darting between trees, ducking low branches, crashing through brush, he had not experienced such exhilaration in a long time. Fully alive and invigorated, he enjoyed the warm blood pulsing through his veins.

When he lost track of the hind, Elinas reined in the steed and surveyed his surroundings to orient himself. The sun had vanished behind heavy clouds.

Even the breeze had abated. As he patted the horse's neck, Elinas realized he'd lost his way.

Should he sound the ram-horn hanging from his saddle to call the hunting party? As he reached for the horn, Elinas' heart stumbled. The melodious singing had resumed, much closer this time.

The high, clear voice, so similar to that of his departed wife, enticed him. Captivated by the strange song, intrigued and curious about what angel could sing so beautifully, Elinas directed his mount toward the source of the enchanting voice. It could not come from an ordinary woman.

Elinas dismounted, tied the horse to a birch, and planted his spear in the soft earth. As he crept silently among bushes, he held his scabbard to prevent it from flapping against his thigh. Driven by the need to spy on the angelic voice, he struggled to control his breathing, brought short by anticipation. All senses in alert, he watched his steps, like a lad venturing on forbidden grounds.

The absurdity of the situation struck him. He owned the forest, so why would he hide? But Elinas could not shake the feeling that he was trespassing. As he moved closer to the melodious sound, he recognized the dark canopy of the chestnut grove, and the spring he used to frequent as a boy.

Concealed behind a hawthorn bush at the edge of the clearing, Elinas held his breath. At the top of the boulder from which the water surged, two great skulls of gray stone looked out on the clearing. A cawing raven flew down to perch on one of the moss-grown skulls.

At the foot of the boulder, inside the oval basin dug into the bedrock by the surging water, a woman reclined, bathing. Her lovely arms rested on the stone rim, and her heavenly song filled the clearing.

At the sight of her smooth shoulders, Elinas held his breath. His heart drummed faster. Could she be entirely naked? His manhood strained the leather britches below the baldric that held his sword. Partly excited, partly embarrassed, Elinas flushed. His blood burned hotter than the fires of Bel.

Glad for his hiding place, he admired her long black hair, wide gray eyes, and delicate arms. The pure notes of her song charmed his ears, surpassing in virtuosity the skillful trills of the larks. The archaic words seemed from a lost language, witnesses of a time when the gods roamed the land.

Could this be Coventina herself, the River Goddess?

Enchanted by the melody, stunned by the beauty of the nude singer, Elinas could not help but notice how different she looked from his departed wife. Where his queen had been tall, blond and fair, the woman in the spring had dark skin and small features. When she stopped singing, the woods remained silent for a few moments, as if waiting for more, and Elinas missed the sound of her voice.

Then the lady rose, splashing out of the water. He admired her small breasts and narrow hips. She seemed young. A servant girl approached the lady, offering a wide cloth to dry her skin. The woman smiled then, and that radiant smile to another made Elinas wish she smiled for him.

Elinas pondered coming forth and talking to her. After all, she trespassed on his private estate. But he remained riveted. Even naked, the young woman had a refined manner, a proud way of holding her head. The perfect proportions of her lean body and her unblemished skin attested to a chore-free life.

This was no slave or peasant lass but a lady of noble birth. Determined to meet her, Elinas decided to wait until she had donned her clothes.

The child servant produced a linen chemise and a silky gown of a royal blue that flattered the lady's dark complexion. The gown rustled when she cinched it with a golden sash. Then she slipped on a pair of leather sandals. Although the dress now covered the graceful body, a radiance still hung around the apparition.

The woman combed her glorious hair and set upon it a crown of wild flowers.

Time for Elinas to come out of hiding. He rose and crossed the clearing toward her. "I do not remember seeing you among my hunting party, my lady."

The lady languidly rose and curtsied.

Reaching the stone basin, Elinas braced a booted foot on the rim. "I want to know who you are, and what you are doing on my land."

The lady straightened and met his stare. "Pressine, Princess of Bretagne, daughter of King Salomon. I travel through this land in search of a worthy husband. And whom do I have the honor to address?"

Elinas smiled, not used to identify himself. "Elinas of Dumfries, King of Strathclyde." A princess would never travel without a male kin and a full retinue, so he asked, "Where is your escort?"

"Bivouacking close by." Merriment played in the lady's eyes. She did not seem at all intimidated by his station. "You said you owned this land, but a sacred spring can only belong to the River Goddess."

"Perhaps. Was that you singing earlier? How beautiful." Elinas wondered whether she had guessed his indiscretion but could read nothing in the lady's eyes. "Strange language, though. I never heard it before."

"The song is ancient." Lady Pressine sat on the stone rim and arranged the graceful folds of her gown. "The River Goddess likes it so much, she often enhances its sound."

Elinas remembered the lady's nude body and yearned to touch her smooth skin. "I believe the singer should be given more credit."

"Thank you." Did she blush at the compliment?

Plucking a fern, Elinas sat next to her, eyes down as he fingered the feathery leaves. "Looking for a husband, are you? But surely, your father knows many rich princes who would consider themselves lucky to marry you."

"None in my native Bretagne, sire." Was it regret in her tone?

Elinas gazed straight into her eyes, trying to guess her thoughts. "How could your father king allow such a dangerous journey? Or is there another reason for your travels?"

Pressine suddenly rose and paced in front of him. "Royal women of my blood do not bow to the will of men." She flipped the hem of her skirt as she turned, then planted herself in front of him. "I follow the signs, trust in the Goddess, and decide for myself which man is worthy of my love."

Elinas realized with a start that he wanted her. He chuckled to cover his confusion.

"What amuses you, Lord King?" Her gray eyes sparkled.

"Love? When did love ever determine marriages? I thought I was the only mistaken fool on that subject." The memory of his departed wife filled him with shame and cooled his lust.

Pressine considered him gravely for a moment. "Love is a powerful force. It has been known to rejuvenate the old, give heart to the warrior, and conquer empires."

"Indeed, I believe it." Elinas tossed away the fern and stood. A hint of suspicion brushed his mind. Something about the young princess seemed odd. But what harm could come from such an innocent creature?

Pressine smiled as if reading his thoughts.

"Since you are journeying through my lands, allow me to offer the hospitality of my castle, where you and your escort may stay as long as you wish." Elinas offered his arm to walk the lady to her camp.

Pressine remained silent and did not take his arm.

At a loss, Elinas explained. "Tonight after the hunt, we are feasting in the great hall in Dumfries, to celebrate Beltane and rekindle the fires."

When she did not react, Elinas wondered whether inviting her was a mistake. He had never let anyone intimidate him before, but the lady managed to shake his confidence. "Your presence would be greatly prized as my guest of honor."

Lady Pressine hesitated. "Beltane can get unruly in the heat of fire and mead. Will my retinue be treated with proper respect? Can I place my good name under your protection?"

Offended by the insinuation, Elinas concealed his annoyance. "I maintain order in my hall, Lady Pressine, but I swear to protect and defend your honor if the need arises."

The lady still gazed at him, unconvinced. "You behave like an honorable man but manners can be deceiving. What guarantees do I have of your good faith?"

"Guarantees?" How insulting. What woman ever asked guarantees from a king? Elinas struggled to keep a calm demeanor. "What kind of guarantee?"

"How about that exquisite sword hanging at your side?" The lady reached for the scabbard and lightly traced the intricate designs of gold and silver.

Elinas snatched her wrist. Could the woman be a common thief? "A lady should know that a warrior never surrenders his sword."

"As you wish." Pressine pulled her hand free. "Farewell then." She walked away.

Elinas started after her. "Wait!"

Pressine turned about and faced him.

In that instant, Elinas realized he cared nothing about the precious scabbard or the jewels encased in the silver hilt, but a warrior's blade was his soul. Yet, Elinas could not stand the thought of never seeing Pressine again.

He unhooked the scabbard from the baldric and held it out. "Take it."

When the lady smiled at him, relief and happiness flooded Elinas.

She hefted the heavy weapon as if it weighed nothing. "I promise to return it before you need it again."

She hooked the scabbard on her sash. Where the heavy blade should have dragged to the ground, it held perfectly in place, as if weightless.

When the lady extended a small hand, Elinas took the offered fingers with reverence and brought them to his lips. They felt smooth and cool under his kiss. His entire body tingled with elation as he offered his arm and guided Pressine's graceful steps toward the white mare brought by a page boy.

Elinas grinned as he lifted Pressine's lithe body into the side-saddle. He reveled in the sweet fragrance of lily when her long hair brushed his cheek.

Lady Pressine adjusted the sword on her hip. She smiled one last time then slowly rode away, the page boy leading the mare and the servant girl following on foot.

After the small party disappeared around a thicket, Elinas shook his head, wondering whether he had dreamed the strange encounter. The sword missing from his side, however, attested to the incident, and he felt glad. Suddenly remembering his thirst, he approached the murmuring spring, took the wooden goblet attached to the rock with a rusty chain, filled it up to the brim, and drank in long gulps. Above his head, a raven cried and took flight.

Startled, Elinas glanced up at the circling bird then laughed as he splashed water on his face and short beard. Never had he felt so fascinated by beauty. He sat on the stone rim, caressing the very spot the lady had touched earlier. For now, he could only think about the captivating siren, and he congratulated himself for extending his hospitality.

The Beltane festivities might not be so gloomy this year, after all, although Elinas did not quite trust his feelings. Something in lady Pressine's presence and behavior seemed a little strange, and he wondered what kind of trouble he might have invited to the castle, along with the beautiful princess.

Chapter Four

After her meeting with Elinas at the spring, Pressine's mind brimmed with hope. She hummed as she rode the white mare back to camp. Gwenvael and the Viking had already folded the tents and readied the caravan. Smiling, Pressine gave the order to move on.

When she took the head of the line, Gwenvael and Bodvar gave her puzzled glances and mounted to ride at her side. The Viking looked silly in the gray robe of a monk, designed to conceal his blond hair and his warrior's physique.

"So, how is the king?" Gwenvael's eagerness betrayed his youth.

Pressine smiled dreamily at the memory of the encounter. "He is dark and handsome, and not old at all." She patted the royal sword hanging at her side. "And I own his soul." Alas, she wished it were that simple.

The caravan followed the wide Roman road at a leisurely pace, through the forest full of fragrant blossoms and bird songs. Child servants on foot flanked the heavy ox carts loaded with sacks, barrels, and richly ornamented chests. Sheep and goats closed the rear, bleating and grazing, as children prodded them forward with sticks.

Despite Gwenvael's pleasant conversation, Pressine's mind returned to the spring and to Elinas. She had known from Ogyr's cries that the king had spied on her before showing himself, but he displayed impeccable manners. He looked young and handsome, but level-headed, and in total command of himself.

Seducing him would take cunning. What if she failed? But Morgane and the Goddess counted on Pressine. She must succeed. Besides, she enjoyed the challenge, and she looked forward to her next meeting with King Elinas of Strathclyde.

By mid morning, the small party emerged from the forest, in full sight of the walls protecting Dumfries castle. The fortified Roman fort stood atop a green hillock dominating a fork in the river Nith. Unlike most forts made of timber palisades, the rectangular fortress had thick stone walls and square towers jutting proudly at each corner.

Cottages spread along the river, while all around, the forest had been cleared to make room for fields and meadows. At the base of the hill, a military camp of many large round tents spread along the bank of the Nith, controlling the stone bridge and the wide Roman way. In a field beyond the camp, soldiers trained with swords and spears.

Pressine halted her mare. It saddened her to say farewell again. For how long, this time? "This is where we part."

Gwenvael turned in the saddle to face Bodvar.

With his single eye, the Viking stared, not at the fortress but at the stone arches of the Roman bridge spanning the river. He said something in Norse.

Gwenvael seemed to grapple with the words then nodded and turned to Pressine. "He has never seen a stone bridge."

"Truly?" She stared at the ordinary structure.

Pressine remembered the many Roman bridges of her native Bretagne. The willows and alders lining each bank also reminded her of home. So did Gwenvael's presence.

"Is this the way you go?" Her voice wavered as she motioned with her chin toward the fork in the road before the bridge.

"Yes." Gwenvael glanced north along the river. "The road leads to the Antonine wall."

Struggling not to shed tears, Pressine changed the subject. "Elinas picked quite a strategic location for his garrison." The stronghold inspired respect for the king of Strathclyde. "From here, he can dispatch quickly to any part of his kingdom."

Gwenvael patted the neck of his impatient bay gelding. "On such a good road, we can reach Dalriada in two days."

"Be careful among the Scots. They do not like Bretons much." Pressine gave Bodvar a sidelong glance. She did not trust the barbarian. "Especially a Breton traveling with a Viking."

"Do not fret, sister. They will respect a Culdee friar."

Pressine rolled her eyes at the Viking's poor disguise. "Even under a deep cowl, he may not fool a Scot."

Gwenvael dismounted, then helped Pressine down from her mount.

He winked at his sister. "Arstinchar, the Viking camp, lies far north in the wilderness. We will not tarry in the towns."

"I wish you luck in your daring endeavor, brother." Pressine pointed to the sword hanging over his gray robes. "I always thought holy monks led sheltered lives, but war has a way of changing things." She embraced him, unable to contain the tears that rolled down her cheeks.

"Be safe, sister." Gwenvael wiped her tears. "I hope for his sake that Elinas treats you well, or he will answer to my sword."

"I will give him no other choice." Pressine forced a smile. Emitting a bird cry, she called Ogyr. Immediately, the raven came to perch on her gloved hand. She cooed soft words, caressing the bird's head, then set the raven on Gwenvael's shoulder. "Keep Ogyr with you. If you ever are in danger, send him to me with a message."

After helping Pressine remount the white mare, Gwenvael hopped onto the gelding and spoke a few Norse words to Bodvar.

The Viking grinned, baring a row of strong teeth. He raised one hand in farewell then prompted his big horse along the northern road. Ogyr cawed a goodbye as Gwenvael followed.

Pressine watched them ride away then turned and led her party over the bridge, toward the imposing fortifications. On top of the gray rampart, watchful soldiers stared into the distance, searching the tree line. No doubt they had been watching her party.

No challenge came from the twin towers or the guards at the Western gate. The soldiers on duty bowed respectfully and let the wealthy party inside. Pressine returned the salute with a nod. To the eyes of a guard, rich ladies and their entourage must always be welcomed and posed no threat to a king.

When Pressine passed under the arch of the main gate, she admired the portcullis that reminded her of the Roman forts in Bretagne. This feat of engineering allowed the heavy iron-clad door to be lowered in case of attack. More soldiers loitered inside the gate. Within the vast enclosure, a well organized set of buildings attested to a lordly way of life.

Admiring the judicious use of the villa and other constructions, Pressine recognized the stone of old buildings in some of the newer structures. Earth and thatch cottages leaned against the inside perimeter wall. Stone buildings and wood shacks lay scattered throughout the castle grounds. A safe and fitting residence for the future High King of Alba. Dogs barked and geese scattered as the cortege streamed into the castle yard.

A boy ran out of the scullery to take the mare's bridle.

Pressine stopped the cortege. "Has the hunt returned yet?"

"No, my lady." The stable boy blushed. "The hunters will not return until mid-afternoon."

Pressine slid off the mare unaided and addressed the lad kindly. "I want to speak to whoever is in charge in the king's absence."

The lad nodded and took off with the mare, leaving her and the entire caravan standing in the middle of the yard.

Pressine sat on a stone bench in the shade of a tall oak. Spreading her riding dress around her, she waited.

Soon, the lad returned with the castellan, a pudgy middle aged man in green trews and tunic, puffed up like a courting pigeon with the importance of his function. Cleanly shaven, with thin lips that never smiled, he scowled as he surveyed the lordly train. This unexpected arrival would constitute a severe hindrance in his busy schedule.

Displaying the bejeweled sword as a token of the king's authority, Pressine stated her legitimate invitation.

The castellan bowed with reluctance. "I shall give orders to make space for you in the women's quarters immediately, my lady."

"I fear this will not do, my good man." Pressine tried not to laugh at his surly expression. "Certainly the departed queen had private chambers. I would think them suitable for a princess of my rank, and large enough to host my entourage."

Obviously appalled by the request, the castellan waved pale hands in front of his face. "The queen's chambers must never be disturbed. My lord king would forbid such desecration."

Pressine realized how much Elinas had loved his queen. But for his future happiness, as well as for the higher purpose of the Goddess, she must execute this sacrilege.

"I shall not hear of any other arrangement. I will take entire responsibility." She held the scabbard for the castellan to see. "This gives me the authority to rule this castle as I please."

"But I will fry in the fire if I grant your request," the castellan protested stubbornly.

Pressine hated to use her special gifts for small things, but it was for the Goddess, and she had no time to argue. The success of her mission depended upon it. She closed her eyes briefly and took a deep breath. *Dear Goddess, give me the strength to convince this stubborn man.* A jolt of raw power ran through

Pressine. When she stared the man down, he averted his gaze.

"Perhaps it can be arranged," the castellan uttered sheepishly, shifting his feet. Then he straightened and motioned to the castle servants gawking at the newcomers. "Take them to the Queen's chambers."

The castle servants quickly led Pressine and her party toward a large building. It faced a twin construction across a small courtyard, and Pressine assumed the similar building contained the king's chambers.

Upon entering the late queen's apartments, Pressine choked on the dust. She marched to the windows and pushed open the wood shutters to bring in light and fresh air. The rooms stank of disease. Spider webs hung from the ceiling.

Obviously, no one had set foot in the place since the queen's balefire. Not even Elinas. So he hadn't dealt with her death, yet. Bringing joy back into the king's life might prove more difficult than Pressine expected.

The chambers had once been lovely rooms, but thick dust covered the faded draperies, the four-post bed and its canopy. Pressine would need more servants to clean up the place.

Another request to the castellan produced the extra help.

While lovingly cleaning and packing away the late queen's personal belongings in a square of rare blue silk, Pressine gave orders to a score of drudges to strip and burn the linens and scrub the place clean. In an hour's time the chambers sparkled with new life, filled with sunlight and bird songs.

The servants then carried her heavy chests into Pressine's new quarters. Opening her coffers, Pressine directed the redecorating. Elinas had mourned too long. Time to shock him back to life. It pained her to cause him such sorrow, but it was necessary. For the sake of Alba, the king must overcome his grief and return to active life.

With the help of many servants, Pressine hung lengths of white and blue silk from high beams to lighten the gray walls, then she spread rushes on the flagstone floor. She hung a white linen canopy over the bed posts and replaced the old bedding with a clean mattress, sheepskins and bright blue blankets. Soon, she had a small fire of fragrant pine burning in the fireplace.

Satisfied with her new decor, Pressine thanked and dismissed the servants and closed the bedchamber door. The smell of baking bread from the outdoor oven reminded her of the upcoming Beltane feast. A horn sounded in the distance. She must hurry before the return of the hunt.

After making sure everyone had left her bedchamber, Pressine congratulated herself for such a successful transformation. She reached for the bejeweled scabbard hanging from a peg. She had one more detail to tend to, and it could bear no witnesses.

Unsheathing the king's blade, Pressine held it to the afternoon light. To think that a sword contained the soul of its owner... Thanks to the special link binding a warrior to his favorite weapon, she could enslave the spirit of the King with a spell. Through the sword she could bind his soul forever.

Now that the time had come, however, Pressine hesitated. Where would the challenge be in seducing a puppet? How would she ever know whether he really loved her? She wanted to measure the depth of her future husband, get a chance to love him for who he truly was. Returning the sword to its scabbard, she decided to wait and try her personal charm first.

A cacophony of horns, barking dogs, servants' cries, and the drumming of hooves signaled the return of the hunting party. Hiding the king's sword under the bedding, Pressine smoothed her long hair and composed herself for the inevitable confrontation. The stomping of boots on the flagstone and the fierce pounding of a fist on the door warned her of the king's foul mood.

Without waiting for an invitation, Elinas stormed into the bedchamber.

Pressine shuddered at the loathing in his dark brown eyes.

"Whatever made you think you could violate the apartments of my beloved queen?" Stopping short in the middle of the room, Elinas glanced around, eyes wide with disbelief.

Pressine struggled to sound casual. "Surely your gracious queen would have wanted these rooms light, warm and clean, even alive with laughter, rather than dark, sealed, and stinking of decay."

The king's jaw tightened under the short black beard as he towered over her. His hands balled into fists at his sides. "I alone decide in my castle." The low voice turned to a raucous whisper, more threatening than the shouts of any battlefield. "I shall not tolerate defiance of any kind under my roof. Restore these rooms to their previous state and leave."

Barely able to slow her heartbeat, Pressine feigned distraction, dusting her blue riding dress. "It simply cannot be done."

"You dare challenge me?" His surprise would have been comical, if not for the menacing tone.

"The old linens were burned," Pressine said with a calm she did not feel, as if lecturing a child. She rose to fetch the bundle wrapped in blue silk and handed it to him.

Elinas looked at it suspiciously. "What is it?"

"Her comb, mirror, distaff, spindle, and other keepsakes." Pressine's waved her hand, encompassing the room. "The apartments themselves will never look the way they did before." She had made certain of that.

The king's eyes, velvety brown and soft this morning at the spring, now burned with the fiery amber of a wild cat's glare. Elinas looked ready to pounce. He snatched the bundle from her arm. "Out!"

Pressine showed none of the apprehension gripping her. The king's heart, beneath the leather gear, had more mettle than she anticipated.

"Remember that I have your sword." She paused, observing the sobering effect of her words. "Only this morning, you gave it to me, swearing you would honor your oath of keeping me safe in your halls. Does a king's word count for so little in Strathclyde?"

"I curse the ill fortune that made me hear you sing, lady." Eyes tightly shut, Elinas tensed, fists at his side, obviously struggling for emotional control. "I should have known that a princess who refuses to bow to the will of men can only bring strife."

Encouraged by the spark of reason returning to the distraught Elinas, Pressine hoped he could now face his grief. "I am sorry if I offended you. I meant no disrespect."

"I have enough Vikings, Angles, Picts and Scots to give me trouble. The gods know I do not want feuds in my home." Stillness made his stare frightening.

Pressine refused to be intimidated. "Will you honor your word and protect me, then?"

"I should throw you to the wolves!" His voice boomed.

"Wolves?" Pressine repressed a chuckle. She loved wolves. "What would your people think of a king who throws a defenseless princess to the wolves?"

"Defenseless?" The king's face reddened.

"Everyone in the castle expects to see me at your side at the Beltane feast. If I do not attend, there will be questions. The rules of hospitality state that..."

"Let them ask," Elinas snapped. "The rules of hospitality do not apply to princesses who misbehave!"

"Please, my lord, do not throw me to the wolves!" Pressine dropped to her knees and grabbed his strong legs, gazing up at him. "I promise to behave like a proper lady and heed all your wishes from now on."

Elinas glanced into her eyes then averted his gaze. "Get up!" he said gruffly. "I spoke in anger. But you better behave as promised."

"Thank you, my king." Pressine rose. Her irrepressible smile broadened and she brushed her lips to his cheek. "Does this mean I may stay in these chambers?"

"I see no reason not to anymore." Elinas pursed his lips and sighed. His slow gaze perused the room. Unshed tears welled in his eyes. "My dear queen's spirit has left this place."

Moved by his emotional display, Pressine bowed humbly. "I shall do my best to please you, my lord. I promise."

Elinas glanced at her riding clothes. "I hope you plan to wear something more suitable for the feast."

"Do not fear. I will do honor to your hall." Pressine curtsied. To her surprise, when she raised her gaze Elinas remained standing, staring at her.

"I need my sword," He said curtly.

"What?" Under no circumstance could Pressine give him back his sword.

"A warrior-king cannot show himself at Beltane without a royal sword." The dark stubble of his beard twitched.

Suddenly grasping the opportunity, Pressine went to the most ornate chest in the room. "If a great sword you need, my lord, a great sword you shall have."

Opening the chest, Pressine nonchalantly furrowed among the gold and silver jewels to retrieve the wrapped Caliburn imbued with the might of the Goddess. When Pressine faced Elinas again, he stared, gaping at the riches in the open coffer.

"What is all this?" He eyed the contents suspiciously.

"My dowry." Pressine slowly unwrapped the sword empowered by the ritual in the stone circle. "From my father, King Salomon of Bretagne, and from my aunt, the Lady Morgane."

The king's gaze took in the other trunks as well. "You could supply a whole army for many years with that much silver and gold."

When Pressine unsheathed the blade, it caught the light and shone blue.

"Who did you say your aunt was?" Elinas seemed transfixed by the sight of the magnificent sword.

"Lady Morgane of the Lost Isle." Pressine presented the weapon to his touch.

"Incredible work." His hands caressed the blade. "I have never seen such flawless steel."

"Like the dowry, it will go to my husband in wedlock." Pressine sheathed the sword and handed it to him. "Would you wear Caliburn tonight, as a token of my good will?"

Elinas gave her a sharp glance as he took the sword. "Do not think this gives you license to oppose or contradict me in any way in front of my liege lords and barons. If you do, I shall have you thrown outside the ramparts in the middle of the night. And the royal Princess of Bretagne will have to contend with the wolves."

Caliburn in one hand the blue silk bundle in the other, Elinas marched out of the bedchamber. After the door closed, Pressine let out a long breath and her shoulders relaxed. Seducing this king might prove more difficult than she expected, but he was worthy, and she enjoyed a challenge.

* * *

The delicious aroma of roasting meat wafted into Pressine's chambers. Through the window, she heard the jibes of the cooks taking turns manning the iron spit above the open fires. Dogs yelped, fighting over scraps. Her discriminating sense of smell told her the hunters had killed at least one deer and a boar. Hungry since she broke her fast at sunrise, Pressine rejoiced at the prospect of such an elaborate meal.

Checking her face in the dark water basin, she smiled. With her hair pulled back under a diaphanous veil, and a gold circlet of gemstones on her brow, she shone like her fae mother had... before turning into a cruel shrew. Pressine shrugged away the disturbing memory.

The white gown, embroidered with gold serpents, had a low neckline that generously exposed most of her round breasts. Her dark eyebrows, misty gray eyes and dark complexion needed no color from a jar. With a heavy gold torc on her throat, a touch of deer musk in the cleft, and silver rings and bracelets from her dowry, Pressine felt prepared to captivate a king.

Securing a precious dagger in the front of her sash, she glanced up at the sound of a soft knock on the door.

"Lady," an unfamiliar male voice called. "Our lord king requests your presence at his table,"

So, Elinas had already graced the hall. Pressine knew it was impolite to be late, but she wanted to make a grand entrance. Opening wide the door of her bedchamber, she found a grizzled gentleman in black finery, who smiled with great poise, and offered a wiry arm.

"Allow me, my lady." The red and black ribbons braided in the white beard moved as he spoke. "My name is Dewain, Baron of Ayre and Royal Counselor." He winked. "May I add that I am dazzled by your great beauty?"

"Pressine of Bretagne." She chuckled, accepting his arm. "Delighted to meet such a charming escort."

They crossed the antechamber, then Dewain led her outside into the fading sunlight. Stepping around muddy ruts, they avoided the detritus around the kitchen midden. The stench, however, could not be helped.

Dewain's beady eyes twinkled with amusement. "I met your father once. In Armorica... long before you were born. You have wandered far from home, Lady Pressine."

"And what brought you here from Ayre, Lord Baron?" The appetizing aroma of venison assailed Pressine when they passed the outdoors kitchen on their way to the main hall. Frantic activity reigned around the two open fires, releasing smoke and delectable bouquets on the evening breeze. Pressine slowed her pace to match the old man's steps.

"I retired early to give my heir a chance to rule." Dewain flashed a quick, toothless smile. "Ever since, I have enjoyed the trust and the friendship of young Lord Elinas."

"Young?" Pressine searched for traces of irony in Dewain's lined face but saw none.

He raised an eyebrow. "By my standards, dear lady, a man of thirty-five, as hardy and vigorous as our king, is indeed very young."

"Vigorous? Really?" The thought brought heat to her cheeks.

From under the oak tree, a scullion gawked at Pressine's shapely figure and she smiled. She had made herself as irresistible as she could, but would it be enough to seduce Elinas?

"Oh, if you talk about consorting with ladies..." Dewain shook his head dejectedly. "Elinas has not done that since his dear queen died. The gods know I presented him with many eligible noblewomen."

"Really?" Pressine wanted to ask how pretty the ladies were but refrained. "So, why is he still alone?"

"Grief... A pity at his age." The old baron guided her around a puddle. "Just a year ago at Beltane, when his queen was alive, he jumped over the fires with the young castle lads. I hope he finds happiness again soon."

"Otherwise?" Pressine sensed great sadness in the baron's deep black eyes.

Dewain sighed. "I fear sorrow will break his spirit."

"That would be a shame." Pressine paused outside the hall's entrance. "What would it take, Lord Baron, for the king to spring back to life?"

The beady eyes blinked then stared at Pressine with renewed interest. "The right woman, dear lady. The right woman can always change a man. I hear you are looking for a royal husband?" Dewain's lips curved into a thin smile. "Rather unusual for a lady to search for one herself."

"Well," Pressine held his gaze, making sure he would understand her meaning. "I am a very unusual princess."

When the door opened wide, Pressine smiled and straightened her frame. She hoped the nervous twinge in her legs wouldn't make her trip. Through the candlelight illuminating the feasting hall, she sensed the envious stare of the ladies upon her, many of them young and beautiful. Strengthening her grip on Dewain's arm, Pressine walked stately as she entered the great hall.

Chapter Five

Elinas stopped conversing with a baron at the high table to stare at the unlikely couple walking toward him. The servants stopped pouring wine. The tinkling of ewers against pewter cups waned. A murmur spread among the crowd, then a hush fell on the feasting hall. Even the hounds looked up expectantly, with lolling tongues and wagging tails.

Pressine stood, framed in the open doorway. The penetrating rays of the setting sun behind her rendered the white silk gown translucent. Dark and lithe, she looked like a golden statue of Aphrodite, her nudity barely veiled, as if a sudden draft could expose her anytime. Elinas had never beheld such a vision before.

A powerful pulse in his loins responded to the sway of her fluid curves. He remembered the naked nymph who sang melodiously while bathing in the spring. The rare sight had occupied his thoughts all day and now made his cheeks burn. He wished he had more control over his emotions.

Still battling his anger at her transgression, Elinas decided to offer a truce in honor of Beltane. Besides, he must admit his late queen would have liked her chambers alive with vibrant colors. And how could he begrudge such a bright and beautiful woman as Lady Pressine?

He admired her willowy walk as Dewain guided her toward the royal table.

When she flashed a demure smile and curtsied, Elinas rose to face her. He discerned uncommon strength in the way she carried herself, subdued yet not subservient. Any prince or king would be proud to have her at his side. He shuddered, guessing that if thwarted, she could also make a ruthless enemy.

She offered her small hand. Elinas kissed the soft fingers. His lips lingered there as ripples of excitement coursed along his skin. A pleasing heat suffused his body. "Would you share the royal cup tonight, noble lady?"

Pressine responded with a radiant smile. "But I might shame you by being less than docile."

"Remember the wolves, my lady," he whispered in her ear as he eased the chair to his right.

She gave a small laugh and sat. "I gladly accept your cup."

Her musky perfume assailed Elinas' senses as her veiled thigh almost touched his brown woolen trews.

"Only one condition," she said coyly. "Dare not turn the cup on me."

Elinas scoffed, both amused and excited by the sexual allusion. Turning the cup would be an open invitation to share his bed. The intriguing princess resembled no woman he had ever known. Setting aside all previous resentment, he decided to trust her... for now. "So, you feel like feasting dangerously tonight? It is Beltane after all..."

* * *

Pressine smiled at the mention of Beltane and watched a young servant refill the silver cup she would share with the king.

Tonight on the Lost Isle, after weaving ribbons around the phallic maypole, the priestesses would light huge bonfires. In the heat of the flames, they would couple with druids, princes, and tribal kings, to honor the Goddess and produce a new generation of future rulers.

Pressine glanced up at her king. Did Elinas know of the ancient custom? She did not regret keeping her virginity all these years for the sake of an alliance in the name of the Goddess. Otherwise, she could have been one of the priestesses offering themselves on the altar stone tonight.

Unsheathing her dagger, Pressine placed it on the white tablecloth, beside the thick trencher of hard shepherd bread. The soft glow of the massive chandeliers, alight with several rows of fat tallow candles, illuminated the richly dressed guests and the fussing servants. A woman gave Pressine a brief appraising glance. Laughter and the din of conversations mingled with the chime of silver and the occasional bark of a hound.

"I welcome your truce, Lord King." Pressine did not mind missing the Beltane ritual. So far, she preferred the extraordinary task of seducing a king.

"What if I meant you harm?" Elinas motioned the servant to leave the ewer on the table and handed the cup to Pressine. Did he plan to get her drunk?

"I can fend for myself if need be, Lord King. I fear no mortal man, only the wrath of the Goddess." Pressine tasted the strong mead, careful to drink on her side of the cup.

"Few still honor the old gods." Elinas took the cup from her and their fingers touched.

"I do." Pressine quickly removed her tingling fingers from the goblet. She found his contact too pleasurable and distracting.

"I once worshiped the old gods. But they took my queen..." Elinas cleared his throat. "Now, I strive to be fair and wise, but I doubt that my reputation spread all the way to Bretagne. What makes you think you can trust me?"

Pressine's surprise must have shown, causing Elinas to smile. She had no answer, just a feeling about him, and she trusted the Goddess.

A young boy ladled kidney stew on the bread trenchers, then a servant girl added creamed beets and boiled dandelion greens. Finally, a cook proudly set a silver platter containing the hind quarter of a deer in front of the king, on the high table.

Picking at the stew with clean fingers, Pressine observed less tidy diners. "To answer your question, like my aunt, the Lady of the Lost Isle, I can read men's hearts. I see in you a generous soul, destined for greatness."

Elinas carved a chunk of deer, dropped it on her trencher then cut another piece.

"I have no great ambition, dear lady. I feel satisfied with ruling fairly, protecting the borders against barbarians, and maintaining a fragile peace among tribal kings and barons. That is quite enough." He bit into his meat with lusty appetite.

"I understand." Pressine cut and speared a dainty bite with her dagger. The sweet meat melted in her mouth, satisfying her cravings.

"You do?" Elinas raised a dark brow.

"Of course. But what about the Vikings? What if they come in great numbers and sweep the land?" She blotted fingers and lips delicately on the hem of the long tablecloth, as good manners dictated.

Elinas threw his scraps to a begging hound. "The Vikings are a pricker in my backside." He drained the cup, refilled it, then returned to the food. "May the gods help us if the barbarians bring whole armies. We could not stop them."

This seemed like the perfect opening. "What if the Goddess helped you unify the land? If you were crowned high king of Alba over the tribes of Scots, Picts and Angles, they would stop fighting each other and bow to your authority."

Elinas groaned as he chewed a mouthful and waved a leg bone.

But Pressine would not give him a chance to protest. "The united tribes could join forces to protect the coast from the Viking threat."

The king swallowed hard, bobbing his Adam's apple. "The old gods have grown weak in this land." With the point of his dirk, he dislodged a piece of gristle from his teeth. "A single king cannot control all the land between the Hadrian and the Antonine walls."

"It could be the only way to repel the Vikings, my lord." Pressine speared a slice of beet. "The Vikings used to strike and run, but now they have strongholds in the Caledonian wilderness. They prepare an invasion."

"I hope not." Elinas waved away her comment. He did not believe her.

"Still, you could unite the tribes to protect the coast from their raids."

Elinas shook his head. "King Alpin of Dalriada would never give me his oath. He would probably like the title of high king for himself, though. I understand he entertains big dreams. I'm glad the Picts keep him busy, otherwise, his Scots would fall on our land like wolves."

Having heard little of the northern tribes, Pressine asked, "How dangerous exactly are the Picts?"

Elinas shrugged. "A bunch of filthy savages. They rape and kill women and children. Every summer, they scramble over the Antonine wall, half naked, painted with blue woad and black pitch. They raid villages and small towns on the northern border, slaughtering indiscriminately for food, gold, and weapons. And all in the name of Christendom."

She drank a sip of mead, feeling suddenly warm. "What about the Angles?"

"The Angles of Lothian?" Elinas wiped the fat from his mouth with a white linen sleeve. "They despise us Britons, befriend the Saxons, and covet our fertile lowlands. As for the Saxons of Mercia to the south, they have not crossed the Hadrian wall for a long time. But who knows when they may decide to ride north in search of new farmlands."

"Really?" Pressine knew all this but wanted him to open up, so she could gain his trust.

Around them, barons and lesser nobles, engaged in conversations of their own. They paid little attention to Pressine and the king, as if to give them privacy.

Pulling his chair back in a grating of wood on the stone floor, Elinas eased Caliburn on his hip and spread one long booted leg in front of him under the table. He sighed, his soft brown eyes on Pressine. "But what is all this to a beautiful woman?"

Although she acknowledged the compliment with a smile, Pressine did not relent. "If and when Alba finally unites, you would want to be in control, making the decisions rather than relying on Alpin of Dalriada or Loth of Lothian."

Elinas raised both eyebrows as if in subtle warning. "What king would not?"

When he brushed Caliburn's hilt with light fingers, Pressine wondered whether he could feel the sword's magic.

She made her voice low and seductive. "So, you do like power."

"I used to, but I do not enjoy it lately, not since..." A shadow briefly darkened the king's gaze.

Realizing the extent of his grief, Pressine hesitated. "Your queen..."

Elinas refilled the silver cup. "She was cheerful and sweet, not as spirited and independent as you, dear lady. The fever took her before the last harvest." He drained the cup, set it down, then filled it again.

"I am sorry she left you so soon." Pressine fell silent. She couldn't imagine the pain of such a loss. She also wondered how it might feel to be loved that much by a worthy man.

Children offered bowls of scented water and wet towels for the king and his guests to wash their hands. More servants brought baskets and gathered the bread trenchers soaked with the juices, and the leftovers of the meal. Later, according to custom, they would distribute these remains among the servants and the poorest of the town people.

After setting fresh trenchers of hard bread on the tablecloth, youths served the second remove of stuffed eggs, blood sausage, and young cabbage. This time, the servants paraded a whole roasted boar around the room, to the applause of the diners. They ceremoniously set the head on the king's table, along with a generous quarter of the beast.

Retrieving his knife, Elinas carved a slab of boar and chewed on it, throwing pieces to the hounds who wrestled them under the table.

"Is your aunt Morgane really Fae? I thought these were legends." He licked the juice from his fingers. "If this is true, King Salomon has unusual alliances. Very few still believe in the power of the Ladies."

"In Bretagne, Lord King, the Goddess favors fae children with extraordinary gifts. The Ladies requested my father's services for a Beltane mating, as is customary." She watched him carefully, wondering whether he understood the ancient rituals.

"And King Salomon agreed?" The casual question gave her no clue.

"Indeed. He was quite taken with my mother and courted her for many years."

Elinas glanced at Pressine appreciatively. "I can understand why, if she looked anything like you."

"Thank you." Heat crept up her throat at the compliment. Pressine wondered whether she had been too bold in her approach. But with this man, subtle behavior would probably go unnoticed. "Father loved my mother very much, but the bishop objected."

The deep brown eyes studied her. "I see..."

"King Salomon repudiated my mother and was punished for it. His Christian bride is barren." Pressine fell silent, unwilling to reveal her own crucial role in the matter.

"Can a Fae marry a king?"

Pressine laughed at the transparent question. "Yes, my lord. It has been done many times."

She considered telling him about the curse but decided it was still too early.

More delicious dishes followed. Then dancers, jugglers, acrobats, and musicians performed. The tumult of voices in the hall grew deafening. Drinking songs and laughter now accompanied the swearing and spitting contests.

Pressine did not participate in these vulgar games and felt glad when Elinas also declined. She considered it bad manners to spit over the table like a hunter. The king cheered his favorite arm wrestlers but did not bet. As for Pressine, she ignored the public wenching that so delighted the male guests.

Elinas laughed and smiled a lot, and Pressine rejoiced at seeing him in such good spirits. Watching him drink, however, she wondered whether he planned a Beltane joining of his own. The lust in his eyes seemed to grow with each cup of mead.

The king made a show of turning the silver cup, to drink where Pressine's lips had touched, a shameless sexual overture.

As much as it was a small victory under the circumstances, Pressine reminded herself that she had come to marry a future high king, not throw her virginity at an imbibed and barely lucid lord. She felt dizzy from the mead and hot as well. In the lewd atmosphere, she flushed under the king's piercing stare.

"Are you afraid of my knowing your thoughts, my lady?" The king raised the cup. "I could use them to my advantage." His smile, devoid of artifice, told much about his hopes.

"My thoughts are yours for the asking, Lord King." Pressine sustained his stare. "But do not summon me to your bed in honor of Beltane. As a royal princess, a maiden of the Isle, I keep my virginity for a noble husband."

"What a shame." He sounded disappointed.

Pressine tried to sound offended. "If you feel such a need, I see many willing wenches in this very hall."

Elinas laughed then set the cup down without drinking. "I have not needed a servant girl since I was sixteen, my lady. And I shall not need one tonight, or any other night."

A glance around the great hall showed that all the legitimate wives had already left. Only drunken men, concubines and serving wenches remained, some of them on the floor, moving in the flickering shadows and making unseemly noises.

Pressine needed some air. "I think it is time for me to retire, my lord."

"Then allow me to escort you to your chambers, my lady. I had enough feasting for one night." Rising on unsteady legs, Elinas offered his arm.

Pressine took it gratefully, unsure whether she could trust him to find his way through the castle grounds at night. With much dignity, Pressine followed the king, stepping over snoring barons passed out from drink, trying not to disturb fornicating dogs and other licentious couples. She tiptoed around pools of vomit, and spilled mead.

When they reached the door and stepped outside into the fresh night air, Elinas gave Pressine a reassuring smile. In the moonlight, he seemed quite sober. She understood then that he was not as drunk as he had appeared in the hall, and relief washed over her.

She smiled and took his arm. As they walked through the dark commons, Pressine felt acutely aware of his strong forearm under her fingers. When her foot buckled on a stone, his other hand came around to steady her waist and lingered there.

"Are you hurt?" He held her close, facing him.

Standing in his grip, close enough to feel his warmth, Pressine relished the proximity of his hard body. "I feel lucky to have such a strong man to keep me from harm."

Both hands on the king's chest, she could feel the pounding of his heart, or was it hers? His linen shirt smelled like heather, and she found herself longing for his embrace. His sword hilt pushed on her thigh. Was he going to kiss her? She suddenly wished he would, and she tilted her chin to meet his eyes, lips slightly open in subtle invitation.

"I am sorry..." Releasing his grip, Elinas gave an apologetic smile. "I should have borrowed a torch from the hall." He looked away.

How she missed his eye contact.

He led Pressine around muddy ruts and rough ground, his arm supporting her waist. Allowing herself to lean upon him slightly more than needed, Pressine enjoyed the contact of his hand through the flimsy dress. She wondered whether he was shy, trying to behave as an honorable man, or still grieving.

Thus linked, they waded among the shadows. A cat meowed on a thatch roof, causing a rat to dart into a shed. Elinas didn't flinch. He exhibited the quiet confidence of those in power, without artifice or pretense. Pressine liked his handsome frame, bright brown eyes, and the quick smile dimpling his short beard.

She had noticed his kindness during the feast, even to the hounds in the hall. Morgane often said that one could judge a man's heart from his attitude toward children, elders, servants, and animals. From what Pressine had seen so far, Elinas stood out as a very good man.

As they neared the kitchen, loud cheers of encouragement attracted Pressine's attention. The two fires on which the meat had roasted earlier, now burned brightly. Around the largest fire, servants and cooks, as well as a few nobles too young for the feasting hall, celebrated Beltane the commoner's way.

Pressine remembered similar customs in Bretagne. "Were the fires lit according to the old ways?"

"Indeed! Lit by a druid from the friction of a fire drill." Elinas removed his arm from her waist as they joined the onlookers forming a wide circle around the largest bonfire.

The king's shyness in front of his subjects surprised Pressine, but she liked his reserve. "Where did you find a druid? So few grace the land in this day of churches."

Elinas smiled mysteriously. "A king has means of finding people..." He cleared his throat. "The castle servants and villagers who helped at the feast will rekindle their own hearth with a brand from these fires, as they do each year."

"We still do the same in Bretagne... although the Bishop condemned the custom." Welcoming the warmth of the flames, Pressine moved closer.

An informal game had started among the gathered men. The king's wide smile told Pressine he enjoyed watching his people at play. She saw no women around the fires, only bantering young men. Scullions and cooks lucky enough to find a mate had long vanished in the shadows. The children conceived at Beltane would be born at Imbolc, as the saying went, in the heart of winter.

"I wager this one wins," the king whispered in her ear, pointing at a blond boy, about thirteen years old, well dressed, and quieter than the men.

Pressine indicated a healthy kitchen lad in his late teens who tied back long dark hair in preparation for the jump. "I bet on that one," she said softly to avoid being overheard.

The young men around the fire accompanied their own betting with rowdy cheers and comments that would make a lady blush... but Pressine had heard it all before.

As she observed the candidates removing their shoes in preparation for the jump, Pressine knew the king had picked the best boy, light, focused, and determined. "What shall we bet?"

"A king never takes gold from a lady." Elinas grinned wolfishly. One eyebrow shot up. "The most fitting wager I can think of would be a kiss. If I win, I shall request one."

So the thought had also crossed his mind! Pressine took a quick breath. Her heart beat faster. "These are very high stakes, my lord." She brought a hand to her chest, struggling to steady her breathing. "And if you lose?"

Elinas looked away. "Then you can set your price, or decide to kiss me or not, depending on how you feel."

Barefoot, the kitchen lad took off at a run. Building up speed, he jumped flawlessly above the flames. Everyone in the circle cheered and applauded. Pressine wondered what she should do if she won the bet. Although she burned for a kiss, it might be wiser to tantalize Elinas a while longer. Realizing she found the king extremely attractive, she did not trust herself to remain cool-headed if the kiss grew passionate.

The younger boy then went to the starting line. Taking one look at Elinas, he ordered the servants to add more logs to the blaze. As they did, sparks crackled, smoke hissed, and the flames leapt five feet in the air.

Pressine watched in fascination, holding her breath, wandering what prompted the boy to act so recklessly. Around the fire, the young men hushed. Elinas turned pale and stared in silence, taut as a bow.

After a last glance at the king, the boy sprinted then jumped without hesitation, clearing the top of the flames and landing safely on the other side. With a smile of triumph, the boy faced Elinas then turned away to receive the delirious praises of the small crowd.

A tear welled in the corner of the king's eye, as he bit his upper lip then smiled.

Surprised by such a display of emotion, Pressine asked, "You know him?"

"Conan." Elinas stated proudly. "My second son. He reminds me so much of his mother."

"A brave boy, determined to impress his father." Pressine wondered whether the tear had been for the son or for the mother.

Elinas sighed. "The dear child just won my bet." He offered his arm to lead her away. "Lady Pressine, you owe me a kiss."

Pressine tensed, unsure how to react.

Visibly enjoying her confusion, Elinas smiled. "But this is neither the place nor the time."

Relieved, Pressine accepted the offered arm and they walked away.

"Whenever I request my due, however, I expect you to oblige gracefully." Elinas chuckled. "I used to jump over Bel's fires, as a young man."

Remembering Dewain's comment about last year, Pressine pictured Elinas jumping the flames. "I wager you still can, my lord."

"Perhaps." Amusement twinkled in his dark eyes. "But I am not drunk enough to try it tonight. Besides, it would be undignified for a king to flop into the flames and singe his britches in front of his vassals."

Pressine joined in his laughter. The stone bench under the great oak looked inviting, but Elinas walked right past it. In the past few hours, Pressine had come to think of him as her future husband, discovering with delight that she truly liked the man. But would Elinas agree to marry her? And how long would he wait before claiming the kiss?

Chapter Six

Back in his chambers, Elinas paced, unable to escape the heat of his rushing blood. The thought of Pressine in the queen's chambers kept him wide awake. How could she have turned his feelings around so fast? He had laughed more tonight than in many months. He probably made a fool of himself, betting a kiss he did not dare claim afterwards.

Not for the first time, Elinas cursed his impulsive nature. Pressine was too young for him, yet her intelligence and maturity went far beyond her years. She had a smart head on her pretty shoulders, and even a sound insight into politics. What a queen she would make some day!

But not for him.

His happy years had come and gone. In these troubled times, he needed to keep his kingdom safe from the Vikings. But tonight, he just could not get his mind to focus, no matter how hard he tried.

Catching sight of a blue bundle on a chair, Elinas stopped pacing to caress the silky fabric. He lifted the bundle and sat on the bed. When he loosened the knot, a whiff of lily of the valley evoked the image of Pressine, rising nude in the spring that morning. He banished the thought. These were his departed queen's precious things.

How carefully each object had been wrapped into the folds, as if not to be damaged or hurt in any way. One by one, a silver mirror, a tortoise comb, a hairbrush of boar bristles emerged from the blue silk. As Elinas fondled them with infinite tenderness, his mind rushed back to the sorrowful time of his queen's passing.

Between convulsions and ravings, in a rare moment of lucidity, she had called him.

"After I am gone, I want you to go on living," she had said with a strained smile. "Promise me to love again and share the goodness of your soul with another woman who can make you happy."

With a violent shake of the head, Elinas had refused to even consider it. "I could never love another."

But the dying queen had pleaded, "How can a king rule justly when his mind is hindered by grief?"

To give her some peace, Elinas had promised, believing he could not keep the oath.

Only now, he understood the wisdom of his departed wife. She had known him well. Had she seen through the pain into the future? Had she chosen a woman to ease his suffering? Elinas smiled sadly.

"Whatever happens, I will always love you," he whispered, as the beloved features faded from his mind. He kissed the silver mirror. "Farewell, my Queen."

Wrapping everything back into the bundle, he tucked it away inside his favorite coffer. He would pass it on to his daughter when she came of age. Elinas realized that his grief would eventually take flight, like his queen's ashes scattered by the wind at her balefire. With time, he hoped his pain would dull to a familiar ache.

How could he be so blind to the natural course of life? Didn't spring always follow winter? He sighed, parting the drapes to look through the open window.

Across the courtyard, Pressine's shutters stood open. A lamp burned brightly on the windowsill. An invitation?

Elinas remembered how Pressine had looked him in the eyes when he caught her from falling, how her breasts had heaved against his chest, how her lips had parted. Had she expected a kiss, then? He remembered the warmth of her skin through the sheer fabric of her gown and wondered how she felt about him.

But Elinas knew how to find out.

If Pressine made his heart sing, what kept him from going to her? He was king after all, and she had wagered freely. Letting the drapes fall into place, he straightened his clothes and smoothed back his hair. Resolutely, he walked out, determined to claim his kiss.

* * *

Pressine ran her fingers over the fine blade, torn between performing the binding spell and letting nature take its course. What if Elinas did not intend to marry her? She tossed the bejeweled scabbard on the bed. He had played with her feelings all night but never bared his soul.

Could she risk failing the Goddess for a matter of simple vanity? Or rather did she fear to discover that her personal charms could not sway a grieving king? How much time did she have before Elinas sent her packing, or went riding against the Scots or the Angles? Border raids always multiplied in fair weather.

And the Goddess demanded prompt results.

Pressine sat on the bed and retrieved the king's sword. For only through the channel of a Lady's magic could Elinas become the instrument of the Goddess, the high king of Alba. She must enchant the blade now, and bind the king's soul. Too bad. She would regret never knowing the depth of his noble heart.

At a slight noise, Pressine turned to behold Elinas two paces away, hands clasped behind his back. He watched her intently.

Her heart raced. "You startled me. How did you get into my chambers?"

"Never mind that. What are you doing with my sword?" Elinas asked in a tone of curiosity rather than anger.

Pressine fumbled to close the silk ties of her open nightgown. "Admiring a fine blade, my lord."

The king laughed. "And this morning I thought you just liked the precious scabbard. How foolish of me."

As he stepped closer, Pressine instinctively moved back, shoving the sword protectively behind her. "Is it customary for a king to visit a maiden unannounced, when all the servants are abed?"

Elinas grinned. The clear brown eyes twinkled above the dark beard as he looked her up and down. "A king does whatever he pleases on his domain. Besides, I came to collect a wager."

At the request, Pressine flushed from head to toe, acutely aware of her nakedness under the silk gown. As she took another step backward, the bedpost stopped her retreat. The king advanced like a hungry wolf, eyes riveted on his prey.

One of the king's large hands came around her back while the other plucked the sword and threw it on the bed, then he lifted her chin. When she met his eyes,

Pressine realized she may not have the strength or the will to refuse him anything. Not tonight, not ever.

Elinas gazed into her soul. Pressine's heart pounded like hammer on anvil. Pulsing heat consumed her flesh where their bodies pressed together. Time stood still as his lips parted and covered hers softly. Pressine enjoyed the prickly beard, the soft, wanton lips, the caressing tongue. Her mind swirled, focusing on the kiss. Touching his mind, she realized Elinas drank life itself from her mouth, his hunger more frantic with each breathless draft.

Eyes closed to lose herself in the sensation, Pressine never wanted it to end. Burying her fingers in his thick hair, she responded in kind, with the pent up passion of an island virgin releasing the flood gate at Beltane. Elinas loosened his grip, but she did not let go of him. A simple taste could not quench her desire.

Finally, Elinas pulled back and stared into her eyes, concern softening his handsome face. "Are you well, my lady?"

Confused and disoriented, Pressine realized that, for a moment, she had lost control. "My apologies," she mumbled, dropping onto the bed, trying to master the new emotions churning in her chest. She closed her gown tighter, wondering whether Elinas despised her now, for wanting too much too fast. "It is my first kiss, my king."

Elinas exploded in riotous laughter. "Your first kiss? You take me for a fool? Such fire..."

Heat rose to her cheeks. Pressine bristled at the implications. "Now that the debt has been paid, my lord, I must ask you to leave."

"In my opinion, you rather enjoyed that kiss." He reached to stroke her arm. "Would you like another?"

Standing up to escape his touch, Pressine struggled to regain control, reminding herself of her duty to the Goddess. "Whether I would like it matters not, my lord. It would be improper. I shall cleave to no man other than my lawful husband. Did I lead you to think otherwise?"

"Is that how you want it?" Elinas flashed an infuriating grin. "Well, we shall see about that." He bowed. "Good night, my lady. Until morning."

As he left, a light spring in his step, Pressine battled the urge to call him back.

* * *

Unable to sleep, Elinas lay in bed trying to get Pressine off his mind. He had serious decisions to make. Should he send troops to defend Galloway? It seemed futile, since one never knew where the Vikings would strike next. On the other hand, he could not forsake a vassal in need.

He found it difficult to concentrate. His mind kept returning to Pressine's kiss. She had clung to him with a passion that left no doubts about her attraction to him. For a brief moment, he even wondered at her claim of virginity. Her confusion afterwards, however, had pacified his doubts.

Making up his mind to consult Dewain before sending troops to Galloway, Elinas finally drifted to a land of voluptuous dreams, full of glorious battles, not all on the battlefield.

He slept through cockcrow but awoke shortly after sunrise, to the melodies of the same enchanting voice he had heard at the spring. Each note, each archaic word, plucked a string that reverberated throughout his entire being. The singing came from across the yard through the open window. Elinas stretched leisurely, wondering whether Pressine bathed naked and sang every morning.

"Something to look forward to," he mused, moved by the lovely picture in his mind.

Getting up in no hurry, he dipped his hands in a pail and splashed water on his face and underarms, rubbed his teeth with coarse salt, rinsed the rank taste of mead from his mouth, then swallowed the salty water. As he donned the fresh linen shirt and green trews spread on the back of a chair, he yelled to the servant who slept behind his door.

"Go fetch Dewain!"

A yawn, then the brush of cloth against wood.

"I will go at once, my lord." The boy sounded sleepy. The pattering of bare feet on flagstone ensued.

Elinas sat on the bed and pulled on the high leather boots, then stood up to buckle his baldric and adjust Caliburn on his hip. Approaching the window, he drew the blade to the morning sun. He had not dreamt the strange radiance last night, by candlelight. The sword did glow with bluish fire. Furthermore, Elinas could feel warmth radiating from the weapon, as if it truly had power.

He knew of great swords forged in antiquity by ancient gods. The bards told tales of ladies guarding such swords in mysterious isles, but Elinas had never heard of a sword named Caliburn.

The heavy door opened, interrupting his thoughts.

"Lord Dewain, Baron of Ayre," the servant boy announced dutifully, allowing the old man inside before disappearing behind the closing door.

Glad to see his friend, Elinas sheathed the blade to greet him in a bear hug. "Dewain, I need your advice."

The old baron winked. "This early in the morning, sire? A matter of great urgency, I suppose?"

"Did I wake you?"

Dewain laughed dryly. "I have been up for hours." He rubbed his elbow. "Old bones loathe the dampness of spring."

The body servant came in, carrying a tray loaded with food, a wine ewer and two pewter goblets, which he set on the table.

Elinas pulled a high-back chair away from the massive table and sat, motioning Dewain to do the same. "Will you break your fast with me?"

"I would be honored, sire." Dewain sat gingerly.

Elinas pulled out his dirk. Breaking a piece of bread, he spread goat cheese on it. "You said yesterday I should take a new queen."

"Indeed! Why this sudden interest in the drivels of an old man?" Dewain's dark eyes twinkled with amusement. He poured dandelion wine in both goblets. "Have you changed your mind overnight?"

"What if I have?" Elinas chewed, savoring the bread and mild cheese.

"So, why do you need my advice now, since you refused it yesterday?" Dewain selected a boiled duck egg then tapped it on the table. He peeled the crumbling shell with gnarled fingers. "I can tell that you already made up your mind."

Elinas drank some wine, enjoying he tartness, and smacked his lips. It had started to turn to vinegar but he liked its bite. "I need to know whether or not Lady Pressine is worthy of a king. Do you believe she is who she claims?"

"Ah... Lady Pressine..." Dewain swallowed and dusted dry egg yolk that trembled in the ribbons of his beard. "I believe she is the daughter of King Salomon of Bretagne. I met her father once, and what she told me is consistent with what I know of him."

"She also has an extravagant dowry... More gold and silver than in my coffers." Elinas rose, walked to the window and stared at Pressine's chambers across the courtyard, trying to shake a disturbing feeling. "Do you think she wants to buy herself a crown?"

Dewain twisted in his chair and faced the king. "If you hope to impress me with her wealth, you are wasting your time, sire. The only question is, how do you feel about the lady?"

Elinas leaned back against the windowsill. "When it comes to my kingdom, I value your opinion, old friend... even though I do not always abide by it. So, indulge me."

"In that case, you have my blessing, sire. Lady Pressine has all the dispositions of a great queen, I am certain of it. As for her womanly qualities..." The grizzled head tilted to the left. Dewain winked. "I have no doubts about them either."

Elinas returned to the table and hacked off a slice of ham with his dirk. "She is so young, Dewain, still a virgin."

"Curious." Dewain chuckled. "I never understood why virginity is considered an asset. But she could be older than she looks."

"What do you mean?"

Dewain cleared his throat. "She has a sound mind for one so young, a good sense of humor, and she shows great promise in navigating the treacherous waters of a royal court. The perfect jewel for your crown, sire."

Elinas suddenly realized that his attachment to Pressine went deeper than he would have thought possible in such a short time. As if by magic, she had rekindled his appetite for life. He could not let her go. If it took a husband to make her stay, a husband she would get.

"It is settled, then. I shall propose this morning. We can be betrothed in a few days and married at midsummer, when Mattacks returns from Whithorn."

Dewain glanced up with interest. "You seem very sure that she will accept."

Unwilling to say more, Elinas allowed himself a mysterious smile. "I have my reasons."

"Ah. Very well." Dewain drummed his nails on the table. "My only worry is your Edling, sire. Mattacks may not see the lady as favorably as we do."

"I know..." Elinas distractedly picked at crumbs of cheese on the table. "Mattacks barely tolerates his brother Conan. He will hate the idea of Pressine usurping his mother's place. She might breed more brothers to dispute his throne."

"Worse than that!" Dewain took a sip then set his goblet down on the table. "He may view her Pagan allegiance as heathen and evil. The old faith is frowned upon in Whithorn where Christians have churches and monasteries. Bishops and abbots preach against it daily. Even in Ayre. They harassed me so much, I left the province to my heir, who is far more accommodating with the Christians."

Elinas stroked the blade of his knife. "I managed to remain neutral so far, welcoming renegade druids and holy monks alike. Bel be my witness, I even gave my Edling a Christian tutor."

"When Bishop Renald hears of a Pagan joining in Dumfries castle, he will hound you both until you convert." Dewain sighed. "And, as sure as I am alive, a Lady of the Isle will never submit to a bishop's rule."

Elinas remembered his conversation with Pressine. "When she says her Aunt Morgane is Fae, what does it really mean, Dewain?"

"It means, sire, that Lady Pressine must have Pagan gifts as well. The Ladies I once knew could weave spells, foretell the future, and demonstrate the power of the Goddess in frightening ways."

Elinas leaned over the table toward Dewain and lowered his voice. "I always thought the Ladies of the Isle were a myth."

"They looked real enough to me when I traveled through Armorica." Dewain's dark gaze took on a dreamy expression. "Extremely attractive. But their most amazing gift is that they never seem to age."

"Really?" Uneasy, Elinas poured more wine in both goblets with a shaky hand. "You knew them well, then, old brigand?"

"I have known a few." Dewain raised his goblet. "But I was young and handsome in those days. They would laugh at my old bones now."

Elinas joined his friend in a toast.

Dewain sipped the wine "The bishop will accuse Pressine of heresy, of dark sorcery, of consorting with the devil, of human sacrifices, or worse. It could mean trouble." He smiled thinly. "But, naturally, a king can hold a bishop at bay better than a baron could."

"Would a bishop dare attack his king?" Elinas planted his dirk into the tabletop, immediately regretting his lack of control.

"Not openly, sire. But do not underestimate the might of Rome. The pope is still trying to rule our country from afar. Charlemagne and his bishops are only pawns."

"Rome is far from here, Dewain, and I can take care of myself."

"I believe it, sire."

"Then it is settled," Elinas said with an assurance he did not feel. "I will propose to Pressine." He shifted in the chair and cleared his throat before breaching the other matter. "Any word from Galloway?"

Dewain's expression sobered. "None since the report of the Viking raid a week ago. Why do you ask?"

"We should not send any spearmen until we hear of another attack in the same area." Elinas rubbed his beard. "The raids are usually random. The Vikings are probably long gone."

"It looks that way, sire." Dewain sank back in his chair. "But we do not know for sure."

* * *

Pressine gazed through the open window at the king's chambers across the courtyard, agonizing over what to do with the royal sword. Against reason, she kept postponing the binding spell. The more she waited, the more she felt attracted to Elinas, but apart from drunken lust in his eyes, she could not read his heart. Her own feelings for him blinded her.

A servant girl erupted into the chamber and ran to her. "Lord Dewain brought this for you from the king, my lady."

"Where is the baron?" Pressine snatched the offered pouch and peered through the open door.

"He left." The girl curtsied. "Said the king was on his way here."

The king had not bothered to announce his last visit. Wondering what prompted such formality, Pressine loosened the strings of the silk purse. Her jaw fell open as she gawked at the heavy gold necklace, a lovely work of art. The polished gold, amber, and jet stones shone as she held the jewel to the morning light.

Her heart leapt. Did the king want to win her love? She kept her excitement in check. Perhaps, Elinas simply wanted to apologize for last night's kiss, or purchase sexual favors, or other kinds of favors entirely. In any case, he had chosen well. Pressine liked the present. It matched to perfection her tan skin and black hair, and the gold tone complemented her blue gown and golden sash.

At a rush of activity in the antechamber, she guessed Elinas had arrived. To present a conciliatory face, she quickly asked the servant to fasten the necklace around her throat, then dismissed the lass. Pressine liked the weight of the smooth gold on her skin. It nestled comfortably between the curves of her breasts.

Elinas strode in and bowed as the door behind him closed. Pressine noticed the ceremonial broach pinning the coat, the feathered hat, and the bejeweled baldric holding Caliburn.

"Why such a formal visit, my lord?" Her fingers flew to caress the necklace. "And what in the name of the Goddess could warrant such a lavish gift?"

Elinas grinned, dimpling his short beard. "I see you chose to wear it. Does that mean you like it?"

"Like it? What woman would not?" Pressine hesitated. "What you may request in exchange, however, troubles me."

"Good!" Elinas took the hat off with one hand. Then he combed strong fingers through dark hair. He looked jumpy as a deer.

Pressine liked his boyish vulnerability under the gruff demeanor. "I thought it took more than a mere woman to make a warrior-king anxious."

"You should give yourself more credit, sweet lady." His voice sounded like a caress.

The familiar address as well as the comment raised the soft down on the skin of Pressine's neck. Had he come all dressed up to ask her to bed?

Pressine indicated a chair, but Elinas just threw the hat on it, unpinned the coat, and spread it on the high back. Then he walked straight to Pressine, forcing her to retreat and sit down on the bed. Dropping one knee on the thick rug, he brought her hand to his lips.

"My lord, what are you doing?" Pressine's heart rammed against her ribs.

Elinas stared into her eyes. "Asking you to be my queen."

Delightful shock and pride at her success suffused Pressine's face. She congratulated herself for not using magic. For her peace of heart, however, she needed to ascertain the king's true motives. "Why this sudden decision, my lord?"

"Does it matter?" Elinas sounded amused.

"It matters to me."

The king's brown eyes softened. "I could tell you that I need the protection of the priestesses of the Lost Isle to save the land from the Viking threat. I could tell you that I want your gold in my coffers, that Dewain wishes me to remarry, that I never really renounced my dream of becoming high king... It would all be true to some extent."

"But?" Pressine held her breath.

"The simple truth, however, is that since I laid eyes on you, my heart started to sing again, and your presence fills my mind day and night. Just looking at you makes me the happiest man in the land, and I cannot imagine life without you at my side. I believe, sweet lady, that the exalted feelings I have for you constitute true love."

Stunned by such an honest and courageous declaration, Pressine fell quiet. Her throat constricted and tears of joy blurred her vision.

Elinas squeezed her hand. "Please, do not delay your answer. If you despise or refuse me, or if I am just and old fool, I need to know it now."

Pressine raised one finger to touch his smooth lips. "I know not how to express what I feel, except..."

Under his expectant gaze, she leaned forward and their lips met in a soft, slow kiss that grew more ardent. Neither of them, however, made a move to take things further.

Finally, Elinas rose to his feet and helped her off the bed. Holding her at arm's length, he asked, breathless, "Do you accept?"

"I would love to become your queen." Pressine sighed. "But on one condition."

"Oh?" Elinas released his grip on her shoulders.

Standing very straight, Pressine smoothed her gown then spoke gravely. "You must solemnly swear that you will never attempt to see me while I am in childbed."

Elinas chortled. "Strange request... Is that all?"

His smile faded as Pressine's anxiety grew. How could she convey the seriousness of her plight?

"As simple as it may seem, if you ever break that vow, the Goddess will strike the land, steal any happiness you may have, take me away from you, and curse your male descendants down to the ninth generation."

Elinas emitted a low whistle. "A curse?"

Pressine swallowed the lump in her throat and nodded.

After a short pause, Elinas gazed into her eyes. "I pledge on my crown that I will never attempt to see you in childbed."

"Thank you, my king. As long as you keep your oath, our happiness and the prosperity of the land will endure." Relieved, Pressine allowed herself a smile.

"Anything else I should know?" The gravity had gone from the king's voice.

"Yes my king, many good things. But we have ample time to discuss them later." Pressine laughed, feeling light as a bird taking flight.

Chapter Seven

Gusts of wind rattled the closed shutters, ushering into the room the sweet smell of fermenting mead. Alone in her chambers, Pressine shuddered with foreboding as a hound howled in the night. A row of tallow candles around the rim of the stone basin illuminated the dark water surface. Pressine bent over the reflecting pool, holding her breath. Would Morgane answer the call at this late hour?

When the flames flickered and smoked, the water rippled, and Pressine perceived a subtle change.

Staring back from the basin, Morgane shifted her gray gaze. She smiled. "I see you remember my lessons, Pressine."

"Elinas proposed," Pressine blurted, unable to hide her excitement. "Betrothal in two days, wedding vows at Midsummer. Will you come? You are my only family in these lands."

"You seem pleased. So, you like Elinas?" Morgane looked serene, as usual.

"He is a wonderful man. I feel so privileged."

A whiff of Morgane's lavender scent emanated from the basin. "I knew you would like him. I am proud of you, child. I will attend the wedding and bring with me the blessing of the Goddess." Morgane's smile faded. "But there is much to do until then. I had a vision."

"What?" A twinge of foreboding clenched Pressine's chest. Visions seldom brought good news.

Morgane's face remained serious. "The Vikings will attack in great hordes. I saw carnage on the

Western shore, south of Ballantrae. In the vision, the moon was but a sliver, making it three weeks hence. Time enough for Elinas to march his army to the coast."

"Will he be victorious?" Pressine's chest constricted at the thought of Elinas going to war.

"From what I saw, it could go either way. Even warned and prepared, Elinas will face a fearsome opponent, but the Goddess favors him." Morgane stared right through Pressine. "In my vision, Bodvar himself led the fray."

"Bodvar?" Pressine's mind whirled at the thought of Gwenvael's gentle soul among the dreadful Vikings. "But he has not yet reached his camp. We parted ways only two days ago."

Morgane shrugged. "His warriors are preparing the attack, and he will lead them despite his promise."

"What about your hostage?"

Morgane looked away. "Bodvar does not believe I can harm his son, or else he cares not. Njal is just a pawn in the gods' game of chess."

"Am I also a pawn in that game?" Somehow Pressine did not find it such an honor anymore.

"Not a pawn, little one, but a queen. Or you soon will be. Good night, Pressine. Remember that the fate of Alba rests in your hands."

As the candlelight flickered again, the water rippled. Morgane had gone, and the shallow basin only mirrored Pressine's worried face. Could she really save the land from the Viking threat?

* * *

Pressine's powers of coercion had no effect on the king.

Boot heels pummeling the flagstone, hands behind his back, Elinas paced Pressine's chamber. He crossed a ray of sunlight alive with suspended dust, then suddenly turned about.

"You expect me to raise an army, ride to Ballantrae through my vassals' lands, and stake my reputation as warrior king on the word of two women who converse through water basins?"

"Lady Morgane wields the power of the Goddess, my lord."

"What if her vision does not come to pass? My chieftains will laugh at me for believing old wives' tales. The Christian barons might even see the work of the devil in this."

Pressine rummaged in her mind for a persuasive argument. "A few days before it happened, I had a vision of the Viking raid on Iona. Then I defeated Bodvar's longships by summoning a sea-serpent."

"You?" Elinas squinted at her quizzically for a few seconds. "I know not how I feel about all that magic." He turned away. "With all due respect, Lady Pressine, when it comes to war, I value training and strategy. I concede that luck often determines the outcome of a battle, but I never directly experienced the powers of the gods."

"You doubt the Goddess?" How could a king refuse her favors? "Why not ask your druid what he thinks of Morgane's vision? Or do you prefer to let Bodvar plunder your kingdom while you make up your mind?"

The king stopped pacing. His expression stilled and his voice rose with menace. "No one is going to steal my kingdom while I live!"

"Then you have to trust me." Slowing her breathing, Pressine focused and grounded herself in calmness. She must convince Elinas. "The Goddess never lies," she said, from the deepest place in her soul. "She favors you, my king, and wants to give you foreknowledge. You should accept Her gift."

The anger vanished from the king's features. "Although I tend to believe you, I could never tell my barons in council how I came by this information."

Encouraged by his openness, Pressine rested one hand on his arm. "My brother is a Christian Friar among the Vikings. He could have relayed the warning."

"A spy among them? Very clever..." The king's hand covered her fingers. The brown eyes softened. "And if the Vikings do not attack, I can save face by blaming the agent, or his circumstances."

"But they will attack, my king, and you must act quickly." Finding the contact of his arm distracting, Pressine freed her hand and took two steps back in order to gather her thoughts. "You must assemble the largest army you can manage, then head for the western coast."

"Since when are you giving your king orders?" The coy smile belied the gruffness of his voice.

"I beg your forgiveness, my lord. Far from me the thought..."

"You seem in a hurry to see me gone." Elinas stepped toward her, impossibly close. "Could this all be a ploy to postpone our betrothal?"

"No." Pressine nestled against his chest. "We can be betrothed before you leave, then wedded when you return victorious. Think of the glory. Alba will see you as the scourge of the Vikings. The Scots, the Picts, and the Angles will look upon you with respect."

Elinas grinned, enveloping her in strong arms. "I never realized, until I met you, how much I relish the taste of victory."

Safe in his embrace, Pressine enjoyed his cheerfulness. "With the Goddess at your side, you will see many triumphs."

His belly laugh shook her body and reverberated throughout the chambers.

"Amazing, how you make me feel young and ambitious again."

"It suits you, my lord." She gazed into his hazel eyes, and as if by magic, their lips met for a lusty kiss.

* * *

Two days later, Pressine's heart beat like a Beltane drum as she left her chambers with a retinue of servants for the betrothal walk to the great hall. As she led the cortege, her long hair, crowned with wild flowers, blew in the breeze. She picked up the hem of her white gown to avoid the mud around the midden.

As a girl, she had often imagined this blessed day. Today, the Goddess would give her a king. But the Goddess would also make him ride to war immediately after the feast. Pressine shivered at the thought. Hard as she tried, she could not foresee the outcome of the battle.

Around her the girls giggled as they walked. Messengers galloped in and out through the western gate. For the last two days, fast riders had dispatched messages and brought the support of neighboring lords. An army a thousand strong, made of nobles, mercenaries, and freshly levied youths, camped outside the fortifications. Other reinforcement from the westernmost provinces would join the troops near their destination.

When her cortege passed the open gate, Pressine glanced at the camp outside the wall. White, red, and yellow tents had mushroomed on the green slopes around the Roman fort. Tribal kings and barons, come to fight the Vikings, would attend the betrothal before going to battle.

Their banners hung above the ramparts and fluttered in the morning breeze. The white lion on a field of azure represented Galloway. Pressine also recognized the three gold crowns of Strathclyde, the red poppy of Mochrum, and the three white stars of Murray. Further along the wall flew more pennants, Cunningham with its unicorn, the black cross of Nithdale, the crimson heart of Douglasdale, and the stag of Ayre.

Pressine led her cortege through the jumble of ox-carts loading supplies from the cellars for the army's journey. Her long flowing hair, crowned by wild flowers, caught the fragrant breeze. The blare of horns and the yells of the cart drivers punctuated her walk.

In front of the great hall, royal guards in red uniforms stood at attention in two straight lines, forming an honor path to the door. At the end of the path, under a bower of white lily, ferns, and heather, stood a gnarled druid in white robes.

Leaving her now silent retinue, Pressine walked the honor path alone.

As she took her place under the bower, she felt like the young virgin she was, waiting for her beloved to formally claim her as his future bride. The ends of the blue and gold scarf at her waist stirred in the breeze. On her throat, the necklace Elinas had given her two days earlier sparkled in the midday sun.

Ladies in their best finery, children and noble guests crowded each side of the path behind the guards, to witness the betrothal. Their sudden hush told Pressine the king had arrived.

Dressed in white, Elinas walked confidently towards her between the two rows of guards. The great sword Caliburn clicked and sparkled on his left hip. How magnificent he looked, trimmed beard and hair raven black. A younger man could not have displayed such poise and bearing.

Even the delicious aroma wafting from the kitchens did not stir Pressine's appetite. Despite her happiness, her stomach knotted at the thought that Elinas would leave immediately after the feast. What if he were wounded, or worse, slaughtered in battle? What if Caliburn failed to protect him? Suddenly, Pressine wished they had made love when they had the chance.

The King took his place under the bower on the other side of the druid who smiled benignly. Elinas gazed upon Pressine and grinned as he took her hand. She squeezed his fingers, returning the smile.

"Let us begin," Elinas ordered.

The holy man bowed then raised both arms and eyes to the cloudy sky. "In the name of Bel of the Dreadful Eye, and Lugh the Shiny One, and Oghma who invented the alphabet, may all promises be kept in this world as in the otherworld, and may a happy marriage follow this solemn engagement."

Chanting an incomprehensible litany, the druid circled the bower sunwise three times. Then he dipped a mistletoe sprig in a pail of water from a sacred spring and sprinkled betrothed and guests. Pressine noticed that he did not name the Goddess. A druid would feel more inclined to invoke male gods.

Mentally, Pressine thanked the Goddess and felt her reassuring presence. When it came to the wedding proper, Morgane would also officiate and make sure the Goddess took part in the invocations.

Then Elinas produced a wide glistening ring. Holding her hand steady, he slid the jewel onto her finger. Pressine realized with delight that the gold, amber, and jet stone matched the necklace he had given her earlier.

"My King, it is exquisite!"

The druid coughed, as if to call everyone's attention. "In the presence of the Celtic gods, I declare Elinas of Dumfries, King of Strathclyde, and Pressine, Princess of Bretagne, solemnly betrothed, to be lawfully wed at midsummer."

Flushed with happiness, Pressine let Elinas slide his hand around her waist and bring her close. His kiss lingered, and he held her tight. Her head reeled, and her legs weakened in his embrace.

Spring flowers showered the couple. The crowd cheered when the double doors of the great hall opened wide behind the bower. Taking Pressine's hand, Elinas guided her inside, then everyone filed in through the bower after them, to enter the great hall.

They sat at the banquet tables, arranged in U-shape, with flower garlands and white tablecloth, like for Beltane. But despite the splendid feast, the mead, and the dandelion wine, the merriment in the hall did not match that of the previous agape. Pressine hardly touched the roasted goat, lamb, fowl or goose. Elinas seemed preoccupied, paying much attention to his generals, with whom he discussed military matters.

As the meal progressed, Elinas dismissed the entertainers, and most of the ladies retired. The celebration turned into a war council, and the charming king metamorphosed into a leader of men.

Fascinated by the aura of power emanating from Elinas, Pressine wondered whether the Goddess had a hand in it. Everyone deferred to the king's wisdom, his cunning, his experience. Even old Dewain seemed to admire his knowledge. Barons and chieftains obviously liked and respected him.

Pressine understood why the Goddess had chosen such a man. In perilous times, Elinas glowed like a beacon of hope. He reminded Pressine of a dragon, wise, mature, dangerous, and full of fire.

* * *

By mid afternoon, the army had assembled in ranks outside the wall, and Pressine struggled to control her tears as she faced Elinas in the courtyard, near the gate.

"Farewell, my betrothed." The king had changed into leather battle gear. Standing by a dappled steed, he blinked against the sun piercing the light clouds and gazed into Pressine's eyes. He seemed unconcerned about the watching crowd.

Pressine's throat constricted, preventing her from speaking for a moment. Warm tears rolled down her cheek, but she forced a smile, for his sake. "I shall stand on the rampart, when you return victorious, my king. I will pray the Goddess to protect you."

Elinas took her chin and gently kissed a tear. "I have one good reason to come back, Pressine. Nothing can keep me away from you for long." The horse at his side shook its mane and whinnied impatiently.

Pressine untied the blue and gold scarf from her waist then slipped it through a leather strap on the king's left shoulder and fastened a knot. "As a reminder that I expect you back, my lord."

Gazing at Pressine, Elinas kissed the end of the scarf. "It will remain on my shoulder night and day, until I return to you."

The king mounted the tall steed, waved once, then galloped through the western gate, toward his army.

The hoof-beats resounded in her chest as Pressine ran up the wooden stairs leading to the top of the ramparts. Shading her eyes from the sun, she watched as the old druid and two priests from the town walked among the departing troops, bestowing similar blessings with twigs dipped in a pail of water. Pressine shuddered. Christian holy water could sometimes be lethal to her kind.

Men loaded the dismantled tents on ox-carts. More oxen pulled heavy catapults of wood, metal, leather and rope. At the sound of a horn, Elinas detached himself from a party of barons to take the lead of the column.

The king rode ahead on the western road, followed by a long line of riders. Soon, they picked up speed and galloped towards the tree line. The infantry marched behind them. Then the train of ox-carts pulling heavy equipment and supplies closed the rear at a sluggish pace.

"Dear Goddess," Pressine prayed, when the last riders had disappeared into the woods. "Please protect Elinas, and victorious or not, bring him back safe and whole."

Chapter Eight

Gwenvael and Bodvar emerged from the woods as the sun dipped in the western sky. Gwenvael straightened in the saddle, stiff muscles screaming for some rest. For many days, he had followed the Viking warlord through rolling hills, highlands, meadows and woods. The barbarian had long since shed his monk disguise and looked like a fierce warrior.

Spring had melted the snow, but the nights remained cold. Gwenvael never complained, even when Bodvar insisted in traveling all day, stopping only to water the horses, and at nightfall to eat and sleep.

The daily stew of hare or partridge, felled from the saddle with a sling, lacked the savor of unavailable herbs, or the aroma of roasted venison. The Viking liked his game boiled in a pot but Gwenvael longed for more flavor in his food. Today, no easy prey had crossed their path. They would dine on stale bread, salted fish, and moldy cheese.

When Bodvar pointed to a towering oak in a meadow, Gwenvael nodded with relief. They dismounted and unloaded the saddlebags. After tethering the horses, Gwenvael gathered dead wood for a campfire. With the branches in place, he knelt to spark a flint stone, then blew softly on the dry grasses he used as tinder.

"Call your bird," Bodvar ordered gruffly in Norse. "I am hungry."

Perched on a high bough, the raven cawed in protest, as if sensing danger.

Gwenvael rose, outraged. "You cannot eat Ogyr!"

"Why not?" Bodvar's single blue eye narrowed in challenge.

"Ogyr is my sister's pet bird."

"Birds are for eating and belong in the pot." Bodvar glanced up at the raven in the tree, then selected a round rock on the ground.

Gwenvael planted himself in front of the Viking to prevent his next move. "You cannot kill him. Ogyr is a friend."

"Animals are not friends." Bodvar shoved Gwenvael aside. "They cannot save your life in battle," he grumbled.

"But this bird can." Gwenvael frantically searched for the Norse words among his limited vocabulary. "He is magic."

Bodvar shrugged, fitting the rock into the leather sling. "Only Odin has magic ravens that tell him the news of the world." He stared at Gwenvael. "And Odin is a great god. You are nothing."

"But this bird belongs to the Goddess!"

Ignoring the comment, the Viking swung the leather straps wide. In desperation, Gwenvael broadsided Bodvar who stumbled and caught himself, letting the rock fly far off the mark. Ogyr flew away toward the woods.

The Viking's hand went to his sword hilt. "Are you denying a warrior his meat?"

Gwenvael trembled. He remembered how, when the rain had prevented all fire, Bodvar had eaten a raw squirrel. Who knew what else this savage was capable of?

Steel rasped against the scabbard as Bodvar slowly drew his sword.

But Gwenvael made no move. He could not win against the Viking. Nevertheless, he stood his ground with bravado. "You'll have to kill me first."

Gwenvael knelt in the grass but kept his head high. *God Almighty, have pity on your humble servant.*

Bodvar's menacing expression turned to disbelief. The big man erupted in raucous laughter that echoed through the nearby woodlands.

"You look meek, but you have the balls of a Berserker," the Viking bellowed between laughs. "I could have killed you."

Daring to hope, Gwenvael swallowed hard then rose. When Bodvar slapped him on the shoulder, he staggered but regained his footing.

"I like your loyalty, even to a bird." The Viking sheathed the sword.

"So Ogyr will live?" Gwenvael held his breath.

"Raven meat is not that good anyway." Bodvar made a disgusted face and dismissed the matter with a wave of the hand. Picking up the sling, he motioned toward the woods. "There is enough daylight left to kill something better."

Glad to be alive, and relieved that Ogyr would not garnish the pot, Gwenvael rushed back to the fire and fanned it so it would not choke.

They had fox for dinner that night, boiled with dandelion greens. By the light of the campfire, Bodvar smiled below the eye patch. He finished the last of the skin then wiped his moustache with one forearm. "No more mead until we reach Arstinchar."

Gwenvael considered the empty wineskin with some disappointment. "God will provide..." He had tried to broach the topic of religion many times without success.

Bodvar planted his knife in the ground and admired the loose wicker frame he had fashioned. Then with great care, he proceeded to slip the fox pelt, like a sleeve, over the frame. "All the gods are barely enough to look after the world. How could one single god possibly do the job properly?"

Gwenvael lacked the words to explain the concept of monotheism. "My god is more powerful than all the Norse gods together."

Bodvar's brow shot up in warning. Then he shook his head slowly and mumbled something in his beard as he smoothed and stretched the skin.

Gwenvael sighed but did not pursue the matter, unwilling to antagonize the Viking.

"Tomorrow..." Bodvar threw his handiwork on the pile of curing pelts collected during the trip and similarly prepared. "We feast and get drunk, and we sleep in Arstinchar."

"Your camp? Really?" Gwenvael glanced around at the moonlit countryside. "All these hills look the same. How do you know we are close?"

"I saw a seagull." Satisfied by his explanation, Bodvar lay down on his sleeping fur, closed his good eye, and started snoring.

Gwenvael slept better that night, knowing that the arduous trip would soon end. The grueling pace imposed by Bodvar had considerably shortened their journey.

Awake before sunrise, Gwenvael saddled and loaded the horses. By the time the sun warmed the dew on the meadows, the two riders had climbed up and down several craggy hills. Toward midmorning, Bodvar slowed his mount and waited for Gwenvael to catch up. He pointed straight ahead, to the northwest.

"Behind that hill is the sea."

Gwenvael stared at the hillock facing them. "How can you tell?"

"A sailor can always smell the sea." Bodvar laughed then made a show of sniffing the breeze.

Gwenvael filled his lungs. Closing his eyes, he could detect salt spray, seagulls, fish, and seaweed. Indeed, the air had a different quality, reminding him of the monastery in Iona.

The two travelers rode on, and by noon they crested their last hill. Shading his eyes, Gwenvael gazed at the scintillating sea.

In the bay, a great fleet lay at anchor. Row upon row of longships bobbed on the waves, sails furled, inside a harbor fenced with a palisade of partially sunken stakes. The sharp points, jutting at a dangerous angle above the surface, forbade any illicit entry or surprise invasion.

Gwenvael estimated the number of ships to about a hundred Drakkars, a dozen merchant longships black from the pitch that coated their hull, and a myriad fishing boats.

At the edge of the bay, a large fortified settlement straddled the mouth of a river. Tall mud embankments, separated by wide moats full of shiny water, guarded the swarming borough. Long houses buried in turf resembled upside-down truncated boats, forming rectangular patterns around central courtyards. Smoke from many hearths fanned into the breeze.

"God Almighty! Arstinchar is no camp. It is the biggest town I have ever seen!" Gwenvael must have sounded like an ignorant farmer but did not care.

Bodvar laughed at his surprise. "Springtime!" he exclaimed. "My brothers have come from Gotland, my home land."

With no other comment, the Viking spurred his big horse down the slope, sending clumps of sod flying in its wake. Ogyr took flight.

Gwenvael sent his bay into a gallop after Bodvar, yelling encouragements to the horse. Lagging behind in enemy territory would be unwise.

The two travelers rode through the southern gate. They crossed the moats on wooden bridges connecting a maze of imposing clay walls. Flat and wide at the top, the walls allowed sentries to walk their lofty lengths.

The Vikings cheered when they recognized their prince. They clanged swords and axes on round shields in an enthusiastic welcome. Those who had no shield brandished their favorite weapon and yelled at the top of their lungs. Soon the noise rose to a deafening din.

Gwenvael felt rather vulnerable among so many barbarians, but God would protect him. After all, he had come to do His work, convert these barbarians to Christianity.

Gwenvael and Bodvar dismounted amidst the clamor. Boys wearing slave necklets led the horses away. Bodvar motioned for Gwenvael to follow him into the central longhouse. Green turf topped the curving clay walls. Bodvar went in, stooping through an impossibly low door, half the height of a man.

Surprised, Gwenvael hesitated. Laughter erupted from inside. When he bent under the lintel to follow, Bodvar mimicked the action of slicing off his head. Gwenvael shuddered.

"Only one entrance." Bodvar winked. "One warrior can defend the house by himself." He shooed away several female slaves who ran into an adjacent room.

"Clever." Gwenvael nodded. *And bone chilling deadly.*

The tiny windows, covered with hide oiled to the point of translucency, could not accommodate even a child's body. Whoever tried to snake through the central smoke hole in the roof would inevitably land into the fire, which burned bright and hot.

On four sides of the central room, a raised wooden platform, like a wide bench, two feet high and three feet wide, served to sit and socialize. Gwenvael noticed the ample storage space underneath, filled with jars, barrels, coffers, and wineskins. In one corner, a pit containing refuse served as an indoor midden. In another corner, a pile of dry dung waited to feed the fire.

The central room had one door on each end, opening into smaller rooms. From the door to the left emerged a beautiful woman with long auburn hair and startling emerald eyes. Although she wore a slave necklet and a dress of rough maroon wool, her proud bearing bespoke a noble birth.

The woman faced Gwenvael, then Bodvar. "What have you done with our son?" she asked, in

Gaelic. Tiny lines of worry crinkled the delicate skin around her eyes.

"Njal is safe, Cliona," the Viking said in Gaelic, with only a hint of foreign accent. "I left him in fosterage to the Ladies of the Lost Isle. My son needs to study his Celtic heritage."

"Thank you for honoring my ancestry, my lord." Cliona bowed stiffly.

Gwenvael smiled at the woman's credulity, certain that Bodvar had ulterior motives. But maybe the woman just played Bodvar's pride. Then Gwenvael realized that Bodvar had spoken in fluent Gaelic. The sly fox understood and could speak the language all along.

A trace of fright froze Cliona's lovely features as she stared at Bodvar. "Who told you about the Lost Isle?"

"My friend." Bodvar clasped Gwenvael's shoulder and winked at his surprise. "From now on, I want you to serve him just as you served me. Now go."

Raising her emerald gaze to Gwenvael, Cliona smiled in a way that made him blush, then she left the room.

Gwenvael wanted to protest the services of the slave but instead freed himself from the Viking's grip to voice his outrage. "So you understood Gaelic all this time? Why did you pretend not to?"

"Just because we Vikings do not write, does not mean we are ignorant. Of course we speak our enemy's language. Even the strongest warrior is useless without cunning." Bodvar grinned. "It made you learn Norse faster, yes?"

Gwenvael struggled to hide his shame at being manipulated. "How many languages do you speak, then?"

"The languages of all the countries where we trade. We learn from our slaves. During raids, we pretend not to understand, so the enemy will speak freely." Bodvar winked. "We hear useful information that way."

Suddenly, everything made sense. In many instances, Bodvar had not reacted as expected because he already knew. He had remained calm and serene among the Ladies. Gwenvael wondered whether Lady Morgane had detected the subterfuge, inwardly smiling at the thought that, perhaps, she had been duped as well.

"Come!" Bodvar walked toward the door. "I will show you around and we must wash up before the feast. Then we can enjoy good food, good mead, and the warmth of women."

Gwenvael's cheeks grew hot at the last comment. He had little experience with drink and none with women. His fostering among the Ladies and his life as a friar had sheltered him from the crude realities of village life. Would he know how to behave if put to the test? He secretly hoped to find out soon.

When he stepped out of the stuffy house with Bodvar, Gwenvael welcomed the invigorating sea-breeze. The day had started to fade under an overcast sky, and the wind blew from the sea.

Bodvar glanced at the sky. "It smells like rain."

Everywhere warriors and slaves busied themselves around smoky fires. The aroma of baking bread escaped from small earthen ovens, while other kilns fired clay bricks. Beneath a lean-to, a sword smith forged a blade. It hissed and steamed as he plunged it into a tub of strong smelling urine.

Further down the main fare, various kinds of meat and fish simmered in large pots hanging from iron tripods over open fires. The sweet-sour smell of honey emanated from large vats of fermenting mead. Strings of herrings hung over a smoky fire.

Gwenvael recognized the reek of a tanning shed as they passed it. A herd of reindeer pastured in a grassy square, watched by children. When he neared the stables, Gwenvael thought he heard the whinny of his bay. He wondered where Ogyr had gone but trusted the raven to hide at a safe distance.

Everywhere, warriors saluted Bodvar with the enthusiasm of a friend or the respect due a prince. The Viking led Gwenvael to a storage longhouse near the harbor. Made of hewn timber, the building had a wide open door, revealing a wealth of trading goods.

"Look," Bodvar boasted, hooking both thumbs in his belt.

Gwenvael stared at riches beyond imagining. Mountains of ivory tusks, fine furs, balls of wool, ironware, grindstones, rope, tallow, masts, bronze anchors, antlers, wooden chests, baskets full of gold, silver coins, jewelry. Leather goods hung from walls and rafters, or lay in piles stacked to the ceiling.

"Where does all this come from?" Gwenvael scanned the building for the heavy coffer stolen during the raid on Iona's monastery but failed to see it.

"Gotland, Osterland, Iceland, Greenland, Vinland... See this?" He picked up the end of a rope hanging from a huge iron hook on the wall, and handed it to Gwenvael.

Heavier than hemp rope, the tightly braided material had a sleek gray texture, like the rigging of the Viking Drakkars.

"Sealskin," Bodvar explained. "The best rope for boat rigging." The Viking took a few steps and lifted from a pile a straight tusk of white ivory, wonderfully convoluted, as if sculpted and polished by a skillful artist. "And this is a unicorn."

"But unicorns are magic and belong to the world of fae. They never venture among regular people." The sheer horror of unicorn hunting chilled Gwenvael to the heart.

"Never seen any myself." Bodvar shrugged and handed the ivory to Gwenvael. "It's the single tooth of a fish called narwhal. Very rare and valuable. The other tusks against the wall are walrus."

As he set the ivory back on the pile, Gwenvael wondered why the storage house was not guarded. Such riches would surely tempt any barbarian in Arstinchar.

"And what kind of shoes are these?" Instead of a flat sole, a long sharp blade of bone protruded lengthwise under the leather footwear.

"These are for sliding on the ice." The Viking took wide steps, moving his arms, as if running in slow motion. "We call them ice-skates. You can also unstrap the bone blade and wear the shoes without them."

A young Viking with long blond ringlets reaching to his ankles stormed into the storage house. His blue eyes twinkled as he smiled brightly. Pink lips and white teeth flashed in a sparse beard. "By Thor's thunder, it is good to see you again, Brother."

As if stung, Bodvar whirled, drawing his sword to strike down the newcomer, but his blade met with the steel of a broad axe. Both warriors held each other's stare, arms trembling under the strain of their powerful lock. The veins at their temples swelled and pulsed, while their faces reddened in a contest of pure strength. Suddenly, both Vikings relaxed and exploded in laughter. Dropping the weapons, they clasped each other in a manly embrace.

"Your speed and strength have improved, Ragnar. Always prepared to defend yourself, even against your favorite brother. You have learned much."

"I had the best teacher." Ragnar winked.

From Bodvar's proud smile, Gwenvael gathered that he had taught his brother how to fight.

Bodvar sobered and his gaze softened. "What news of our father?"

Ragnar gave Bodvar a puzzled look then glanced at Gwenvael. A Culdee friar with a fuzzy tonsure and no slave necklet would indeed raise suspicion in a Viking settlement.

"You can talk." Bodvar sat himself on a pile of furs. "I owe him my life."

Ragnar flashed Gwenvael a quick, wolfish grin then returned his attention to his brother.

"King Alrik's health is good enough, but the young men of our beloved homeland are restless. They grow tired of Gotland's long winters and poor crops. The reports of plunder and rich lands in the south and the west are tempting."

Gwenvael could not believe the barbarians would so casually divide the lands of Alba like a prize.

"New hordes, commanded by young nobles, take to the sea each spring. Many never return."

"And what prompted you to leave our father's hall?" Bodvar's brow shot up.

Ragnar sighed. "I came to carve myself a kingdom. You were right after all. Our father has too many sons."

"A pack of wolves! Killing each other for his kingdom. One day, they will kill him, too." Bodvar spit as if to avert a curse then relaxed into a smile. "But there is enough land in these isles for both of us. I plundered Britannia for ten years and the loot only gets better. Welcome to the land of plenty, Brother."

Gwenvael's gasp went unnoticed by the two Vikings, too engrossed in their rejoicing to pay attention to him.

Ragnar's blue eyes twinkled. "I brought a great army. Tonight we celebrate, and tomorrow we sail south to find me a summer kingdom. I would be honored if you joined my raid."

Bodvar smiled widely. "With pleasure. A warrior gets rusty when he does not fight. Which lands shall we conquer?"

"The lowlands just south of the territory occupied by the Scots." Ragnar spoke fast, with the enthusiasm of the young.

A shadow crossed Bodvar's forehead. "Are you sure that is the land you want?"

"It is the best suited," Ragnar explained. "And the most vulnerable kingdom, if my spies told the truth."

After a short hesitation, Bodvar rose. "Then you shall have it!" He clapped Ragnar's back.

Gwenvael barely contained his rage. How could Bodvar plan to invade Pressine's kingdom despite the promise he had made to the Ladies?

"Tonight, we feast." Ragnar squeezed Bodvar's shoulder then walked out of the storage house.

"What about your son, Njal?" Gwenvael could not believe Bodvar's treachery. "You left him with Morgane as a hostage. What will happen to him?"

"Nothing." Bodvar laughed. "Women would never harm an innocent boy."

"But you gave your word!" Outrage strangled Gwenvael's voice.

"A warrior must take advantage of every circumstance. Things change." Bodvar stepped outside. "I will take you to the sauna. I shall see you later at the feast."

Stunned by the betrayal, Gwenvael fell silent. Dispirited, he followed Bodvar through the settlement, wondering how he could warn Pressine of the upcoming raid. He had to find Ogyr.

* * *

Pressine's heart rejoiced at the sight of Gwenvael's reflection on the calm surface of the water basin. Surrounded by naked Vikings in a cloud of steam, he submitted to a slow massage by young females in scant clothing. Pressine smiled at his shyness. He looked well, even strengthened by the long journey, judging by the added muscle on his wiry frame.

Pressine wished Gwenvael could see her, or at least hear her thoughts, but her brother had renounced and lost his gifts to embrace the Christian faith. She should be grateful he survived baptism. Even now, he searched for a way to warn her, unaware that she had witnessed the conversation between the two Viking princes. Although she did not grasp their language, Pressine had followed their thoughts. Their duplicity only confirmed Morgane's prediction of the coming raid.

Not far from Gwenvael, a stout warrior straddled a lusty lass. Uncomfortable, Pressine erased the image with a wave of the hand. The water surface misted over.

When it cleared again, the basin reflected the beloved face of Elinas. Sitting in council amongst his barons, he looked grave, preoccupied, restless. Pressine's heart went out to him. She missed him, wishing she had followed him to war, but she knew quite well that the king would refuse to place her in any danger. She sent him thoughts of love, woven in a spell of protection.

Elinas relaxed and looked up, straight at her, surprise in his eyes. "Pressine?" Not a question, but a cry of delight.

Overwhelmed, Pressine realized that he had felt and recognized her presence. Warm currents of energy poured from her whole being toward the man she loved. He now looked happy and full of vitality. Suddenly Pressine understood why the Goddess had chosen Elinas. From a faraway past, traces of Fae blood flowed in his veins.

* * *

Back to Bodvar's longhouse, Gwenvael berated himself for refusing the slave's sexual advances in the sauna. Where did he ever get the notion to save himself for a special woman? Or was he simply afraid of displaying his inexperience?

In the end room assigned to him, Gwenvael unpacked his meager bundle. Since he had no clean clothes, he gladly accepted the Viking attire the lovely Cliona had laid out for him.

The woolen leggings, hemp shirt, leather jerkin, and laced fur boots were big for him but felt comfortable enough. The sword, however, hampered his movements. Not only did he have to carry the awkward weapon at all times, but Bodvar wanted him to practice sword fighting.

Gwenvael sighed. What could he do in his present situation but conform? Perhaps, he would grow from the experience.

Careful not to be noticed by the slaves in the adjacent room, Gwenvael furrowed among his possessions. He found some parchment and cut out a small piece with his knife. He pulled a quill and black ink from his pack then scratched a short message. After blowing to dry the ink, he tucked the message into his shirt.

He could not call the raven. That would attract unwanted attention. Later, he would find Ogyr, affix the note to the raven's leg then send the bird back to Pressine.

"What are you doing?"

Gwenvael jumped at the sound of Bodvar's voice. He had not heard the Viking's stealthy entrance and wondered how long he had been standing there.

"Just unpacking my things," Gwenvael stuttered, wiping sweaty hands on his trews.

"You are not trying to warn your sister with filthy writing, are you?"

"Of course not." May the Christian god forgive his lie.

"Good. Otherwise I would have to kill you."

Gwenvael strained his lips in what he hoped looked like a smile. "That will not be necessary."

Bodvar spit over his shoulder to avert evil. "Writing is strictly forbidden. And spies are not beheaded like warriors, but hung from a pole like thieves, until they rot to pieces, pecked by the birds and weathered by wind and rain."

No wonder the storage house had no guards! Gwenvael shivered. God Almighty, let them not discover the truth. He smiled bravely.

"Is it time to eat? I am starved." But his stomach tied into knots, and his throat felt so tight that he could not swallow a pea.

Bodvar grunted and motioned for Gwenvael to follow him into the large central room. There he asked three slave girls to accompany him to the feasting hall. Then he told Gwenvael.

"Each warrior must have servants to cater to his every need." The Viking motioned to Cliona. "You take her. She is your slave from now on."

Gwenvael realized that he had never owned a slave before and had never needed one. It felt wrong to have total power over a kindred soul who had committed no crime. Besides, Cliona was a princess, and a decade older than him, as well as Njal's mother.

Cliona smiled in approval though, and stooped out of the longhouse.

Bodvar followed with his women, then Gwenvael joined Cliona outside. Dark clouds obscured the setting sun, forerunners of a storm. Sudden gusts heavy with sea spray whipped their faces. Head down into the wind, they made their way towards the feasting hall.

Cliona seemed pleased. She smiled engagingly every time Gwenvael glanced at her.

When they entered the chieftains' hall, Bodvar slapped Gwenvael's back. "You seem to like her. I am glad. I bedded her for many years. You will enjoy her."

Heat burned Gwenvael's cheeks. So, the gift did imply sex. At his obvious embarrassment, the Viking roared with laughter. Cliona smiled. Evidently, she had known all along and expected that much. Gwenvael now understood her sweet, submissive attitude. It was all part of a slave's duty.

They sat on the raised platforms surrounding the earthen floor of the chieftains' hall. At the central fire pit, male slaves finished preparing the food. The slave girls sat behind their masters, within reach. Bodvar took the place of honor against the back wall, Ragnar to his right, and Gwenvael to his left. Loud thunder clapped overhead, silencing the rambunctious crowd.

As if on cue, Bodvar rose. "Thor's thunder is blessing our expedition. Victory will be ours." Raising his mead horn, he yelled, "Luck in battle!" then drained the horn.

"Luck in battle," a chorus echoed. The assembled generals and bravest warriors drained their horns as well. In the heat of the moment, so did

Gwenvael, but he wondered how long he could keep up with this rowdy bunch.

When male slaves brought platters of food, the noise in the hall intensified. It failed, however, to drown the rolling thunder, the wind, or the downpour of the tempest raging outside.

Chapter Nine

With a shiver of disgust, Gwenvael refused the platter of steamed raven. Please, God, make sure Ogyr is safe from these savages. After hours of feasting, Gwenvael's stomach churned with shark meat, reindeer, bear, horse, lamb, seaweed, pea-flour bread, and puffin eggs. As he made an effort to sit straight, his head lolled like a cork floating in a turbulent sea of mead.

In the chieftains' hall, the overwhelming stench of smoke, urine, and sour vomit now superseded that of the food. Heavy raindrops, falling through the smoke hole in the roof, hissed and steamed in the central fire. Among the Vikings sprawled on the wooden platforms, the conversations had degenerated to near altercations.

Gwenvael found it difficult to ignore the lewd behavior of the warriors. He needed some fresh air. Attempting to stand on wobbly legs, he fell on his rear. He should not have drunk so much.

"Cliona!" Bodvar bellowed, through a mouthful of lamb. "Help him!"

The slave had already stepped forward to support Gwenvael, who struggled to remain dignified despite his awkward position. As he stood up, with Cliona's help, something from inside his shirt fell to the floor in front of Bodvar.

The Viking stopped chewing and picked up the folded bit of parchment with greasy fingers. "What is this?"

Cold dread sobered Gwenvael, who stared at the incriminating evidence, the note he had scribbled earlier to warn Pressine of the imminent invasion. The Viking prince unfolded the message, then turned the note different ways. The hall grew quiet as the chieftains stopped eating to watch their leader.

Bodvar squinted. "Written words are bad luck!" He motioned Cliona to come close. "You can read. Is it your language? What does it say?"

The lovely Cliona read the small parchment in silence and gasped. She glanced at Gwenvael who stared back, powerless, then she turned to Bodvar. After the slightest hesitation, she declared, "It is a love note, My Prince."

Relief washed over Gwenvael, glad to have found an ally.

"Really?" Bodvar's blue eye narrowed in suspicion. "To whom?"

"To me, I think, My Prince." Cliona did an excellent job of looking embarrassed. "There is no name."

"Read it to me!"

After clearing her throat, Cliona enunciated in a clear voice, "Your fiery hair makes my skin burn, and your cool emerald eyes pierce my heart like Aphrodite's arrows. I long for a kiss. Will you answer my love tonight?"

Still uncertain of his fate, Gwenvael watched the Viking Prince intently. A fly buzzed in the silent hall, landing on Bodvar's meat, but the Viking paid it no heed.

"This is nonsense," Bodvar scoffed. "A warrior can satisfy his need with any slave, anytime, without asking." The Viking shrugged. "If that is what you do with writing, warriors have no use for it."

"But writing can also be used for tallying," Gwenvael protested, now feeling obligated to defend his culture.

"Our merchants have runes for tallying. Since you are living with us, I forbid you to write. Written words are bad luck. They can be used to cast spells. I do not trust them."

Bodvar took the note from Cliona, threw it into the central fire, then spit over his shoulder. "I am too drunk to punish you this time, but no more writing."

"I promise," Gwenvael said in a trembling voice.

When Bodvar returned to his meal and the ministrations of his slaves, the voices in the hall rose again as the conversations resumed.

Cliona squeezed Gwenvael's arm. "Shall I help you out, master?"

"Thank you, Cliona, but please do not call me master." He leaned on her for appearance's sake, although, sobered by fear, he could now stand on his own. "Take me to the longhouse."

Cliona guided him toward the exit, through various human obstacles, some snoring, others copulating in rhythm to the swaying candlelight. Gwenvael enjoyed the contact of her arm, and the movements of her lithe body under the simple clothes.

Outside, the cold downpour washed away the remains of the mead from Gwenvael's mind. The torches under the eaves had fizzled long ago. Arstinchar lay in utter darkness between angry strikes of lightning.

Once away from the chieftains' hall, he straightened and turned away from Cliona to relieve himself. Then he walked silently at her side through the rain. As they approached Bodvar's longhouse, Gwenvael slowed his pace.

"Thank you for saving my life. Bodvar could have killed you for it."

"I am glad I could help." Cliona's smile made her eyes sparkle through the dark rain. Drenched strands of hair stuck to her lovely face. "But slaves are too valuable to kill. When they misbehave, they are flogged, then sold in faraway countries."

Stopping in front of the low door, Gwenvael laid a hand on her arm. "Still, I owe you my life. Does any other lass in the house speak Gaelic?"

"No, they come from the eastern continent and speak a harsh Saxon dialect. Only Bodvar understands our language." She ducked under the low lintel.

"Good." Gwenvael followed her inside, glad to be out of the storm, dripping on the hard-packed earthen floor. He sat on the raised platform bench, unlaced his fur boots, unbuckled the sword and started removing the soaked jerkin.

Cliona stoked the central fire.

"You are drenched. Give me those." She spread them on a cross-beam to dry.

Gwenvael smiled his thanks. "You are wet, too."

She shrugged and stepped onto the wooden platform, then led the way to their private room. Gwenvael followed her in his shirt and trews, unsure how to behave. When she lit the tallow candle on the high window sill, the small and cozy room, with its wooden floor covered with a rug, almost felt like home. The sleeping pallet in a corner looked inviting.

She motioned towards it. "Get into the furs."

As Gwenvael hesitated, she smiled warmly. "Don't be shy. Tonight, we must become lovers. Otherwise, Bodvar might suspect something."

Why did Cliona's words make such wonderful sense? When she gently pulled off his shirt, a shiver rippled through Gwenvael's chest muscles. Standing in front of her, he felt his manhood stiffen when she dropped a light kiss on his bare shoulder.

"I appreciate your sacrifice, Cliona, but I cannot accept it," he forced himself to say, brushing her cheek.

"Sacrifice? Be careful, Gwenvael, you could hurt my feelings. Do you not like me?"

Her hair smelled like clean rain as she leaned against his chest. Gwenvael caressed her wet hair.

"Yes, I like you. You are the most beautiful woman. I feel invincible when you are with me." He wrenched himself away from her. "But as a slave you are obligated... That would be wrong."

"Believe me, Gwenvael, I would not offer this if I did not want it." The emerald eyes gazed far away, beyond the clay walls. "You remind me very much of my late husband. It was a long time ago, in Ireland."

She turned to look him in the eyes and smiled as she deliberately removed the brooch holding her dress together. Her wet garment fell to the floor, revealing a lean body with generous breasts and flawless ivory skin. She was lovelier than the Madonna herself and Gwenvael prayed God would forgive the sacrilegious thought.

Suddenly, he became conscious of his own inadequacies. "There is something else you should know."

"What?" Cliona stepped closer, slowly, sensuously. "Do not tell me you took a stupid vow of celibacy. I heard it is a new trend among Frankish monks."

"No, not that." Gwenvael chuckled despite his embarrassment, but he had no control over the growing bulge in his trews. "I just never... you know."

Cliona reached for the string at his waist. "You mean, handsome as you are, you never had a woman before?"

Gwenvael's cheeks burned as his last garment fell. "Never."

Cliona took his hand. "Be unafraid. You will like it." She led him to the pallet piled with sheepskins. "I promise."

She slid into the skins and pulled him close, covering their naked bodies with soft furs. Gwenvael's fears vanished when her embrace closed around him. He felt safe... and incredibly happy.

* * *

Dumfries castle

"Quick, my lady! There was an accident!" a child yelled running out of the milling shed. It was Mirren, the king's oldest daughter.

Pressine dropped distaff and spindle and left the group of women spinning under the walnut tree to run toward the shed.

"It's Jared, my baby brother." Frantic, Mirren waited at a distance, panting, blue eyes wide with alarm. "His leg is caught under the quern stone."

Cries of consternation erupted among the other women now catching up with Pressine. The wet nurse made the sign of the cross. Why was the shed wide open when not in use? Pressine would reprimand the castellan.

Upon entering the shed, Pressine took in the child's predicament. On the flat grindstone, a small boy of about six lay, pale and silent, as if a prince weren't allowed to cry. A tiny boy with great courage.

Pressine gazed into the big brown eyes locked on hers. Jared seemed to avoid looking down at the leg that disappeared under the heavy quern stone. The wheel-shaped quern, temporary lifted off the flat milling stone for cleaning, had broken its ropes, crushing the boy's leg under its great weight. Fresh blood oozed and pooled on the gray granite.

Pressine noticed Conan, throwing his frail weight against the heavy stone. "It takes an ox to move the mechanism, Conan. Get one harnessed right away."

Prince Conan nodded then darted toward the cow-byre.

The other women gathered around the milling stone.

"A lame prince is a bad omen for the whole dynasty." The wet nurse crossed herself again. "Could be the devil's work."

"Third in line, he is." The castellan's wife shook her head. "As if it is not enough to be landless. He will never catch a good bride."

"May have to amputate..." The plump baroness still carried spindle and distaff, and kept spinning out of habit. "What a shame at such a young age. He will die of putrefaction for sure, like the shoemaker's wife last summer."

"Do not talk like that, you are scaring him." A young girl about fifteen patted Jared's head. She took the boy's hand. "Do not worry, Prince Jared. Lady Pressine knows what to do."

"This would have never happened when his mother was alive." The wet nurse sneered. "She gave strict orders to bar the milling shed. She adored her children."

"Enough!" Pressine boomed. Why couldn't these matrons refrain from making nasty comments? "Make yourself useful or leave."

The women gasped.

Grateful for the silence, Pressine could finally think. "I need boiled water, clean bandages, some clove from the spice cabinet, a fresh cabbage... And get me pieces of wood the size of shutter slats. Take everything to my chambers."

"I shall fetch the clove from the castellan," the compassionate lass offered. Tall and fair with wide blue eyes, she seemed the only one with her wits about her. "And I shall stop by the kitchen garden for cabbage."

Kissing the child's head, the lass hurried out of the shed.

The other women came out of their daze and went to fetch the things Pressine had requested.

When Conan returned, directing the ox with a stick, he harnessed the beast to the beam jutting from the center of the huge stone wheel. Then he slapped the bovine's rear, yelling encouragements. Grudgingly, in a grinding moan, the heavy quern rolled off Jared's leg. The foot looked intact, but from the thigh below the tunic's hem to the ankle bone, only a bloody mess of slack, sickening flesh remained.

"Great Goddess," Pressine whispered, "help me save his leg."

With great care, Pressine wrapped the leg in a flower sac. The boy whimpered and trembled against her body when she took him gently in her arms. Praying the Goddess all the way, she carried him like a baby, careful not to jar him on the way to her chambers.

Once in her bed chamber, Pressine laid Jared on a servant's pallet. From one of her chests, she retrieved a small vial and dripped three drops of the strong mushroom extract on the boy's tongue to dull the pain. The boy relaxed almost instantly and fell asleep.

Soon the women brought bandages and a vat of boiled water, still steaming from the cauldron.

"The water is too hot. Cool it by dumping it in another vat then back and forth." Did Pressine need to explain everything? "I do not want to scald him."

The lass returned, out of breath. "The castellan refused to open his spice cabinet, but when I told him he must save the little prince, he finally gave me five heads of clove." The lass opened one hand to display her prize. "He said to be careful with it. Spices are more expensive than gold."

"You did well." Pressine half smiled. "What is your name?"

"Ceinwyn, my lady. And here is the cabbage." The lass dropped it on the table. "What should I do now?"

"Take some of that hot water and boil the cloves to make a potion," Pressine explained. "I'll chop the cabbage's heart finely to expose the juice, and save the largest leaves for wrapping."

Ceinwyn nodded and set about hanging a small pot of hot water on a hook above the embers in the fireplace. Steam surged and hissed as water spilled on the incandescent coal. Then the lass added the cloves to the pot. "And what will that do?"

With the dagger always tucked in her sash, Pressine sliced the cabbage. "The potion will prevent the blood from going bad, and the cabbage, applied to the open wounds, will keep the flesh from spoiling."

After stoking the fire, Ceinwyn joined her at the table and pulled her own knife to help. "What about the crushed bones?"

Pressine glanced at Jared who lay inert. "We shall set them straight and pray the Goddess that they heal without deformity. The boy is young and his bones are still soft. But he may limp for the rest of his life," Pressine mused aloud. "Unless..."

"Unless what, my lady?" The wide, intelligent eyes gazed into hers.

"Nothing. Just a thought." Pressine concentrated on chopping the cabbage, knocking the blade on the wooden table in a regular staccato. "Since when have you been interested in the healing arts, Ceinwyn?"

The lass glanced up. "It seems since forever. But how did you guess, my lady?"

Pressine smiled. "I can see the eagerness in your face. Would you like to help me with Jared?"

"Yes... I would love to." Ceinwyn beamed. "Would you teach me?"

Kneeling by the pallet, Pressine pushed a vat of tepid water toward Ceinwyn. "Here. Use a clean rag."

She demonstrated as she spoke. "Gently wash all the grime, the bits of meal, and the drying blood, so we can see the wounds."

Ceinwyn followed Pressine's directions as they worked side by side. Once the leg was clean, they applied the shredded cabbage and wrapped it in the leaves. Then they immobilized the leg between two slats of wood and secured it with bandages.

Ceinwyn lifted Jared's shoulders. His head lolled as Pressine offered him the clove potion to drink.

"Bitter." Jared slurred the word but drank some of the brew. He grimaced then fell back on the pallet.

Pressine and Ceinwyn spent the night watching over the young prince. In the middle of the night, while the lass dozed in a chair, Pressine approached the pallet quietly. She wished Ceinwyn had returned to the women's quarters, but it was too late for that. Now she hoped the girl would remain asleep.

Pressine could do one more thing to help the child's recovery, but she could not display her gifts to the common world. If it be known that a heathen could work miracles, Christian fanatics might accuse her of consorting with the devil. Unclear about how the Goddess would view her act, since Jared wasn't part of her mission, Pressine would accept the consequences. She could not let an innocent child suffer.

Bending over the sleeping form of Jared, Pressine laid her hands over the knee joint and focused her thoughts. Her palms tingled from concentration, and heat surged through her fingers. While channeling the might of the Great Goddess, Pressine whispered old words of power in a long lost tongue.

The sleeping child stirred but did not wake. For an instant, Pressine clearly saw through bandages and flesh the crushed bones of the delicate articulation retaking normal shape. Then the vision faded. With a sigh of satisfaction, she covered the feverish child with a blanket and kissed his forehead.

Exhausted by the effort, Pressine dropped onto her bed and fell asleep.

* * *

Each passing day, Elinas grew less confident in Pressine's predictions. What if Morgane had seen wrong? He feared the consequences of his military leap of faith. Too many unknown elements... not enough hard facts to throw at his generals, and no control over a myriad possible events.

Yesterday, however, the scouts had found the battleground described in details by Pressine. Somewhat reassured, Elinas had set camp just out of sight, behind rolling hills. Still. As he faced the chieftains and barons assembled in his tent for the final battle preparations, he wondered whether or not the Vikings would attack.

On the trestle table, Elinas unrolled a parchment. He indicated flowing lines on a rough map. "We are here, where the two rivers converge and flow as one into the sea. The confluent, one league inland, is sheltered from storms and tides."

"These Northerners are good strategists." Dewain's voice, still strong despite his age, rose over the drone of comments. "It is the perfect place to set a military base from which to invade, by land or by waterways."

Elinas tapped the spot on the map with one sturdy finger. "I believe they will bring the longships inland through the estuary, to this fishing village, the one at the bottom of our hill."

"Why not block the river to prevent them from sailing inland?" The naive question came from a young Earl, obviously a stranger to the battlefield.

The generals glared at the man who dared question his king.

Elinas smiled at the young noble's lack of experience, relieved to recollect that the Earl held no commanding post. He attended the council only by privilege of birth.

"If we build an underwater barrier," Elinas explained patiently, "the enemy will only sail further north or south. We need to trap them inland and humble them, or they will keep coming back."

A scar-faced general from Galloway drummed his fingers on the trestle table. "What if they retreat back to the boats and down-river at the first sign of ambush?"

"That is why we must destroy their fleet first." Elinas pointed to the estuary on the map. "With the help of local fishermen, we are stretching strong nets and drag ropes along the bottom at the narrowest point. After we let the longships sail into the estuary, we pull up the ropes tight to prevent escape. During the battle, the wreckage of the Drakkars sunk close to the nets will plug the river and prevent any ship from leaving."

"I doubt they will want to escape." The slick baron in fancy silk looked like no warrior, yet Elinas had seen him fight with the agility of a wild cat. "They could overwhelm us on land. An enemy is most dangerous when cornered."

"They are fierce." Elinas nodded, remembering reports of raids. "But they are on foot and do not expect our archers and our catapults. They have no heavy weapons, no cavalry. Our horses can plough through their ranks, causing great damage... and instill some fear."

A minor chieftain raised one eyebrow. "From what I heard, these barbarians do not know what fear is!"

"Every man knows fear." Elinas had his doubts, but wanted his men to remain confident. "We hold the element of surprise, since they expect no resistance from the villagers. Our numbers will probably even out once the reinforcements from Ayre arrive, which should be within the hour."

The general from Galloway rubbed the scar on his cheek. "My troops are better trained than your fresh levies. Perhaps I should attack first."

"No." Elinas hoped his generals would obey orders. "We start with the catapults as planned. And my archers are accurate with flaming arrows."

Galloping hoof beats came to a halt outside the tent. Conversations ceased as the councilors turned to the open flap. Bursting in, the messenger ran to the king and knelt.

"Sire, a great fleet with striped square sails, about five miles north, approaches fast on the tide." As if just remembering, the soldier added, "and our reinforcements just arrived."

So, Pressine had spoken the truth. The war had started. Elinas gazed at his generals with renewed determination. "Do you all understand your orders?"

Many nodded, others voiced their acknowledgment.

"Get your men in position, and stay out of sight behind the hilltops at all times. The enemy should suspect nothing until I order the attack.

After the councilors left, Elinas indulged in jubilation. A surge of new respect for his future bride suffused him. Not only was she beautiful and loyal to his land, but prescient, intelligent, and dependable as well. She deserved his trust, and he could now let himself love her unconditionally. It felt good, as a king, to have someone upon whom he could rely.

After indulging in a moment of dreamy reminiscing, Elinas focused his thoughts on the coming battle. He had to prepare himself. According to Pressine, he faced a bloodbath.

* * *

Gwenvael leaned over the Drakkar's prow, looking to port, toward the coast of Alba. The land where his sister had gone to become queen... the same land Bodvar's brother coveted. The northern wind billowed the sail, thrusting the bow through the waves, splashing sea-spray on his face. The afternoon sun had disappeared behind clouds, and the sea looked opaque, almost solid under the longship.

Once or twice during the voyage, Gwenvael had spotted a raven circling overhead. Was it Ogyr? He felt terrible about failing to warn Pressine, but what more could he have done under the circumstances?

"What ails you, my friend?" Bodvar towered over him, his good eye drilling him down. "You should be happy to see familiar land again. Tonight, we set camp in Alba."

"You shouldn't do that." Gwenvael realized the futility of his warning but had to try. "No one angers the Goddess and goes unpunished. Although I worship the Christian God, I would not risk the Ladies' wrath."

Bodvar dismissed the comment with a wave of the hand. "I am not afraid of women."

"I remember you thinking otherwise when you saw that monster, Nidhogg, rising from the deep." Gwenvael allowed himself an ironic smile.

"Do not say that name." The giant's broad face paled. "It brings bad luck."

Bodvar spit downwind, into the waves slapping the prow, then quickly averted his gaze from the sea, as if to evade the monster's evil eye.

He stared at Gwenvael. "You saved my life that day, and I am grateful. But never say that name to my face again." His tone left no room for protest.

"As you wish." Gwenvael's gaze searched the coastline. "But the Ladies will fight back. They have strong magic."

Gwenvael did not say it, but he would not be surprised if her sister had an army waiting ashore.

Bodvar's blue eye glared for a moment, then the giant rose to scan the coast. "Except for my brother Ragnar, no one knows where we are going, not even me. How could the ladies possibly find us?"

"They have the sight..."

Bodvar shrugged but looked uneasy. He barked orders for his men to tack, then walked on steady sea-legs toward the stern where Ragnar stood, also studying the shore.

After a few words with his younger brother, Bodvar returned to midship. "Almost there." He turned to his men. "Get your weapons ready, in case we have to fight." Then he casually walked away.

The last remark gave Gwenvael a chill. It dawned on him that he might have to take up arms against his own kind. Caught between diverging loyalties, his sister on one side, his vow to convert Bodvar and free Cliona on the other, what could he do?

Falling to his knees, Gwenvael prayed the Christian god for guidance. After a while, calm and reconciled with his god, he rose and walked up to Bodvar.

"I refuse to fight," Gwenvael said with a bravado he did not feel. "It is my sister's land. I can help you build your camp, serve as a translator, establish trade routes, even collect taxes, but I refuse to kill my sister's people."

Bodvar's brow knitted. "Would you rather fight me?"

"I do not want to fight at all." Gwenvael's legs weakened as he struggled to stand his ground. "I am a Christian monk, not a soldier. I vowed to stay with you until you convert to my religion, that's all."

Bodvar scoffed. "A warrior has no use for your pitiful god. How weak is this Jesus, letting his enemies nail him to a cross! First you worshiped a female god, now a weak god. No wonder Britons cannot fight."

"I hope to change your mind some day." Gwenvael calmly unbuckled his sword belt. "In the meantime, I refuse to use a weapon against my kindred."

He handed his blade to Bodvar but the Viking did not reach for the offered weapon.

"You are crazy, my friend, crazier than the Berserkers in Ragnar's ships." Shaking his head in disgust, Bodvar walked away.

Still holding the sword, Gwenvael wondered what he would do if it came to a battle.

Chapter Ten

From a shelter of trees crowning a hill, Elinas surveyed the confluent. Against a cloudy sky, in the gray afternoon light, the Viking fleet glided into the estuary. About eighty Drakkars, half furled, sailed toward the abandoned fishing village, in the crook of the Y formed by the two rivers. The inhabitants had fled at first sight of the sails.

Elinas signaled the troops to remain quiet. Only the snorting of horses and the occasional clicking of weapons intruded upon the cries of seagulls. Despite the carefully planned trap, Elinas cursed under his breath. He had underestimated the enemy numbers. Was that the reason for his dread?

As he scanned the forested hill north and south, he could not see the troops of Galloway and Ayre but knew they waited for his signal. The catapults stood on the slopes, camouflaged by green saplings and branches.

The large fleet stretched along the river, then split at the confluence to line both shores of the village, just as Pressine said they would.

Sails now furled, the wide-bellied ships thrust their dragon heads onto dry sand, in jagged rows. Amazing that such shallow boats could be seaworthy.

Holding his breath, Elinas waited.

The Vikings poured out of the boats, as if from huge black pods, bristling with barbed weapons, wearing metal helmets and armor plates. On the beach, a big man with an eye patch strode watchfully from boat to boat. He barked orders and posted sentries.

Warriors drew planks from ships to shore and between ships to allow easy access from one Drakkar to the other. Then they unloaded the boats, lit fires on the beach, and carried on the routine activities of making camp.

Still, Elinas waited. He wanted the enemy to feel safe and lower their vigilance.

Some Vikings dug trenches, while others made for the forest, probably to check the surroundings, and find wood for fires and fences. Elinas would not let them venture far... just far enough to slaughter them out of earshot.

When the isolated Vikings entered the forest, Elinas gave a brief order. Surrounded and outnumbered the Vikings took a volley of arrows from archers hidden in the trees. Several giants fell with a surprised look on their faces. Most of the bolts, however, glanced on metal plated shields.

Uttering foreign curses, the remaining wanderers rushed at the Britons with such fury that the spearmen fell back in confusion. Thankful for the thick forest muffling the sound of the skirmish, Elinas galloped into the fray. The Britons, heartened by their king's example, overwhelmed and slaughtered the Viking stragglers. Muted cheers welcomed the easy victory.

Elinas raised his sword. "To the catapults!"

At the signal, a score of men scrambled to remove the branches camouflaging the heavy war machines positioned on the hill the previous day. The huge contraptions of heavy timber and ropes could hurl a stone twice the size of a man's head with great destructive force. But Elinas did not expect accuracy from the old Roman design.

A soldier fitted a stone into the receptacle of the spoon-like arm, while others cranked the lever to draw back the long arm in a moan of twisting ropes. The catapult released, with a thump of the swinging arm against the padded crossbar.

Elinas followed the projectile expectantly. It whistled overhead, hurled into the Viking camp, and crushed a pile of cargo. Another stone collapsed the roof of a shed, causing the thatch to ignite upon the hearth below. Barbarians scurried out of the burning shack. Soon, a steady hail of stones hit the enemy positions on the shore, breaking masts, wrecking ships and obliterating lives. The Vikings ran for cover.

"Archers!" Elinas commanded.

A line of archers marched out of the trees to set up on the slope just below the catapults. Each man carried a crossbow, arrows, and a cooking pot of burning pitch. The archers lit their arrows, fitted them into the slot, aimed, then let fly the first volley. A few darts fell off the mark, quickly extinguished by the river. But bright flames soon licked the inner ribs and the masts of several longships.

Cheers erupted among the Britons.

"Shoot before the smoke obscures the targets," Elinas shouted, cutting off the cheers. Fortunately, the smokescreen would also impede the enemy archers, already at a disadvantage at the bottom of the hill.

Fire rained on ship after ship, swiftly spreading to other Drakkars across the bridging planks. Fanned by the wind, the flames rose, eliciting a flurry of activity on and around the longships. When yells and screams from the boats rose up the hillside, Elinas kept his excitement in check.

Soon, black smoke engulfed the river banks.

A good start for the battle to come. "Switch to sharp arrows!"

The archers launched a volley toward the Vikings rushing up the hillside toward the catapults.

"Sound the charge!" Elinas signaled with his sword.

A horn blared. At the sound, the cavalry galloped downhill, past Elinas who remained at his observation post.

Then he ordered the infantry charge, and the spearmen rushed out of the woods after the cavalry. Three hundred foot soldiers clamored their new battle cry.

"Death to the Vikings!"

"Bring forth our allies!" Elinas ordered abruptly, his impatience communicating to the steed, who shied under him.

Messengers spread out at a gallop toward the various generals.

When a herald sounded the horn for the second attack. The forces of Ayre galloped from the north and Galloway's cavalry from the south, converging on the Viking camp.

Utter confusion seized the enemy. Elinas saw no discipline or organization among them. They neither formed ranks nor spread evenly to meet the attacking waves. Each barbarian fought for himself, compensating for lack of strategy with foolish bravery or individual cunning. Such reckless behavior... Elinas dared to hope.

The Vikings met the horses head on. Uttering bloodcurdling screams, they punched the beasts' noses and hammered down the mounts. They drove swords, axes and spears into the horses' broad chests and underbellies, eliciting rivers of blood.

Elinas flinched at the slaughter. The frightened whinny of the dying warhorses mixed with the cries of agony from the wounded men. Soon, mounds of dying animals and soldiers surrounded the Viking camp at the base of the hill.

"So much for inspiring fear," Elinas muttered, cursing himself for the useless carnage. Since the barbarians disregarded the respect due to horses in battle, he had provided them with a protective wall of horseflesh, and lost half of his cavalry.

Half way between the Viking camp and the tree line, Elinas spotted a score of Vikings rushing toward him. Stark naked, bare-headed, unprotected but also unhindered by armor, they slew every Briton in their path.

The mad men carved a gap in the Briton ranks and spilled through the breach. Elinas grew cold. He had heard of the crazy ones, lusty for battle, oblivious to pain. The barbarians called them Berserkers.

The mad warriors raced straight for the archers and the nearby catapult... or did they aim for Elinas?

"Archers!" Elinas shouted, steeling himself for the assault.

The archers let fly a volley toward the Berzerkers. Several bolts found their mark. But even wounded, the mad warriors kept rushing forward.

A herald blew a horn. Peril to the King! About time...

Troops rushed toward Elinas from all directions. But the Berserkers ran faster, now too close for arrows. Drawing swords, the archers engaged in man to man combat. A losing battle...

One archer threw his pan of burning pitch at a Viking's head. The man caught fire but kept charging. Flaming and screaming like a demon, the human torch rushed blindly, battle axe in hand, straight for Elinas on his horse.

The dappled gray reared and bucked and threw Elinas. He fell hard in the grass. His sword had flown out of his grip. Scrambling on all four, he retrieved Caliburn just in time to block a deadly blow. Then he rose and met the Viking's broad axe in a clang of steel.

Despite his blazing face and arms, the Berzerker did not relent, swiping in wide arcs with the double-edged axe. Elinas glimpsed an opening and slid Caliburn under the man's chin. Only after his crispy head had rolled half-way down the hillside, did the Berserker fall and drop the axe.

Now surrounded by a raging fight, Elinas peered through the smoke. Screaming for courage, he let battle frenzy heighten his senses. He threw himself at the enemy, hacking right and left, engaging every Viking in sight.

Projectiles flew from slings. Enemy or friendly, he could not tell. The Viking devils threw axes. The barbarians fought viciously, with battle hammers and spiked iron balls swinging from maces. They often switched hands, as skilled with the left as with the right, making it difficult to predict their next move. Relentless as killing demons, they never seemed to grow weary.

From the corner of his eye, Elinas caught a glimpse of light on steel. Whirling around, he countered the crushing axe blow from a grimacing madman whose eyes bulged. The Berserker's snarl froze when Elinas cut him wide open below the breast plates.

In the king's hand, Caliburn seemed to fight of its own volition, light, strong, precise, like a living thing. Warmth flowed from the blade to his arm, shielding him from pain and battle weariness. Armed with such a weapon, Elinas felt invincible.

Men ran in every direction, Britons and Vikings alike. Spilled pitch burned along the line where the archers had stood. Wounded men fell into it, rolling in the grass in a futile attempt to quench the flames licking their body. Some ran, screaming and blind, and impaled themselves on enemy blades. Heralds, standard bearers and messengers lay dead or dying.

Thunder clapped overhead. Smoke darkened the sky. Was it the gloaming, or just stormy skies? Having lost track of time, Elinas could not tell whether it was day or night. On both sides, fighting men strained the limits of human endurance.

* * *

Choking on the smoke of many burning ships, Bodvar shouted orders from the deck of his Drakkar. But no one obeyed, too busy fighting or snuffing out fires.

"Cut loose the burning vessels to save those still intact!"

Finally someone heard him over the din and the word spread. More men carried his order from ship to ship. Bodvar shook his head at the disaster. A score of Drakkars had already burned to the waterline and sunk.

The Berzerkers' raid on the Briton commander had almost succeeded. What Bodvar needed now was another chance. He had no doubt that this formidable enemy, with war machines and mounted soldiers, could be defeated if they lost their commander. Individually, the Britons were lousy warriors, farmers, no doubt, and not very strong ones.

Almost as bad as Gwenvael. The Viking glanced at the young friar, who stared at the carnage, transfixed. How could the half wit have warned his sister? With his cursed writing? But how could the lad have known exactly where Ragnar would land? There must be an explanation, and Bodvar would get it out of him, one way or another.

Unless Gwenvael had told the truth and magic was involved. Bodvar wondered about the Ladies' power. Had they truly raised Nidhogg? Were they responsible for this botched invasion? It would not be the first time in history that unearthly forces defeated fierce warriors. Bodvar spit over the railing for good measure.

Amidship, he recognized Ragnar leaning against the ballast. The young Viking kicked a dead Briton overboard. The body splashed in shallow water on the river's sandy shore. Black soot dripped from Ragnar's face in rivulets of sweat. Rage filled the young Viking's pale eyes.

Ragnar set down his weapon to tie back dirty ringlets whipped by the wind and shouted, "Stop worrying, brother."

Everywhere Bodvar looked, the incendiary arrows and the war machines had done their ghastly work. A horn sounded in the distance. Overhead lightning flashed and the thunder rolled.

"Listen." Bodvar pointed to the sky with his sword. "Thor is on our side. Let's show these land-crawlers how Vikings fight."

With a flicker of a smile, Ragnar retrieved his battle axe and dropped down to the beach. "He who kills the most generals gets to keep the best slaves!" the young man called to the wind, before running to the melee.

"And the loser buys the mead!" Bodvar jumped off the boat after him, as the first drops of rain hammered the foredeck. He thanked Thor for extinguishing the fires with a downpour.

* * *

Night had fallen and the barbarians still attacked. The fight had moved away and Elinas leaned against a tree trunk, catching his breath. He saw exhaustion in his men, but the Vikings remained strong. The heavy rain dampened the fires and shortened the range of the catapults. The soldiers defending the big machines would not hold long.

A lightning strike illuminated the battlefield. The fighting had spread, and the Vikings fought best one on one. Trapping them on land might not have been the best plan after all.

Elinas found comfort in the fact that the enemy fleet had suffered great damage. Very few vessels remained undamaged. He could not tell which side had the advantage, though. The staggering number of dead and wounded, strewn on the shore and the hillside, gave no clue.

As the depleted cavalry regrouped in the rain around Elinas, an aide brought back the dappled gray who had fled after throwing him.

"Tell the catapults to stop firing when we enter the enemy camp," Elinas ordered.

He mounted the warhorse and sounded the charge with his silver horn. Spurring the gray, he raced ahead of his brave men.

In a maelstrom of drumming hoof beats, yelling to encourage the horses as well as the men, the meager cavalry swept upon the Viking camp. Hacking at limbs and heads, they trampled in the mud the dead and the dying, wielding swords and spears with ferocity.

In a swift assault, the Britons reached the longships. Soon, the riders found themselves surrounded by enraged Vikings, bent on defending their only means of returning home, the Drakkars.

Thunder rolled overhead, unsettling the horses. Elinas used his steed as a weapon, rearing and sending deadly hooves flying to enemy heads. When he finally saw fear on the Vikings' faces, he took heart. The speed of the attack had shaken the barbarians' confidence.

A young giant with blond ringlets to his ankles, drenched from the rain and sooty from the fire, came at a run along the line of wrecked ships and engaged Elinas. Anger darted from his pale eyes as he stared in defiance, axe at the ready. The warrior's determination sent a chill down Elinas' spine. It felt personal, as if the two of them had a grudge to settle.

The young Viking grabbed the bridle at the bit, forcing the gray steed down on its flank. Elinas leapt to avoid being crushed, then planted his feet in the sand and faced his tall opponent. As Elinas rushed his enemy, soldiers and warriors gave them a wide berth. Despite the barbarian's youth, the gold at his neck marked him as a leader. He certainly fought like one, too.

Hammered by sheets of torrential rain, Elinas dodged the axe, stepped aside, then swept Caliburn upward, but the young Viking countered with unexpected speed. Whoever said battle axes were clumsy had never fought this man. Elinas secretly admired the barbarian's exceptional skills. Blow after blow, they kept hacking. Neither weakened but neither prevailed.

When Elinas thought he could not last much longer, a sudden surge of blue energy flowed from Caliburn to his sword arm. The radiance emanated from the sword. Could it be the Ladies' magic? He thought of Pressine and felt her presence.

With renewed vigor, Elinas rained blows on the young giant, now too hard pressed to counterattack. Rage kept the Viking going, but his strikes weakened. In a matter of moments... There. The opening Elinas had hoped for. Like quicksilver, Caliburn slashed, then stabbed. The young man collapsed in a flood of crimson diluted by the rain, spilling his steaming guts onto wet sand.

A battle cry made Elinas whirl about. A one-eyed madman charged him with a Scramasax, the one-edged Frankish sword. Narrowly deflecting the blow, Elinas engaged his formidable opponent. This Viking, older, battle scarred and battle wise, used his fury with masterful control.

The single eye, cold as steel, daunted Elinas. Already bleeding from multiple cuts, the filthy devil, quick on his feet, delivered strong blows and moved with cunning. Elinas prayed the sword's magic had enough power to defeat such a warrior.

He shuddered as he heard the distinctive hiss of flying stones. The catapults? Against orders?

* * *

With the strength of despair, Bodvar fought the enemy leader. How could a land-crawling Briton have killed his younger brother? At least Ragnar died in battle and now rode to Valhalla in company of the Valkyries. One should rejoice for him. But Bodvar only felt rage. He would not rest until he had avenged his brother's death.

The Briton wielded his double-edged sword with uncanny accuracy. If not for his smaller size, dark hair, eyes, and beard, he could have made a decent Viking. Bodvar switched the Scramasax to the left hand, his right arm weary from too much fighting.

Although he'd learned to compensate for his single eye, Bodvar could not evaluate with precision the depth of his thrust. Once again, it fell short. Even a fraction of an inch could prove crucial against such a skilled warrior.

Taking advantage of his superior size, Bodvar drew his opponent in a contest of strength. Squinting through the downpour, he battered the Briton who blocked his blows two-handedly. But the superior steel of Bodvar's Frankish sword could endure any punishment.

The scramasax suddenly snapped under the Briton's blade. Bodvar screamed as the enemy gashed his left arm. Drawing his dagger with the right hand, Bodvar sought the Briton's central line in hopes of stabbing a vital organ.

Unexpectedly, the Briton turned and ran, just as an eerie sound screeched on Bodvar's blind side. Turning, Bodvar howled at the enormous stone. It impacted his left shoulder in a thud of flesh and splintering bone. As if in a dream, Bodvar fell slowly and watched the stone crash a few feet away. Then he blacked out.

* * *

From the foredeck of the damaged flagship, Gwenvael squinted through the thinning rain. The fighting had ceased. The din of battle had quieted, replaced by moans and whimpers. Had Elinas left? Or would he order to finish off the wounded Vikings?

Like a shadow, Gwenvael dropped to the beach. As a monk, he felt an obligation to give the last rites to the dying who wished for it. Shivering in his wet clothes, he moved among the human charnel, looking for a sign of life, a labored breath, a moan, a plea for help.

The beach crawled with the wounded and the dying. Too many soldiers were beyond his help. Gwenvael blessed those still alive but already gone in spirit, Britons and Vikings alike. He also prayed over the corpses. In his silent quest, he met another priest.

The two exchanged a quiet sign of the cross, then went separate ways.

Among the dead, Gwenvael recognized the mutilated body of Ragnar with his long blond ringlets. He prayed for him, too. God Almighty, in His infinite love, might choose to forgive an ignorant murderer.

A grunt attracted Gwenvael's attention and he hurried in that direction. In the dark, his feet bumped into sprawled arms and legs. He hoped the moaning man would want to confess and be saved.

When he knelt to look at the man's face in the faint glow of waning fires, Gwenvael let out a cry of surprise. "Bodvar!"

The scarred Viking lay shivering in the rain. He had lost his eye patch and his twisted face told much about the pain he must feel. He bled from many wounds, but his left shoulder looked like a hellish mess of protruding broken bones and lacerated flesh. In the midst of that agony, the man found the strength to smile.

"Gwenvael," Bodvar said in a rasping voice. "Odin be praised!"

The strain must have been too much, because the Viking closed his eye and would have looked dead, except for the slight twitch in his gashed arm.

The thought of joining the Britons after his blessing of the dying had brushed Gwenvael's mind, but he knew he must not. He had promised God to convert the barbarians to Christianity. So, he must save Bodvar, who represented his only hope to influence the Vikings' beliefs. Besides, he had also vowed to free Cliona from slavery.

Scanning the beach for help, Gwenvael saw no able body close by. He did not want to attract the Britons' attention to the fact that a Viking prince still lived. The flagship stood two hundred feet away... He had to try.

Jaws clenched with the effort, Gwenvael took hold of Bodvar's feet. He dragged the heavy burden across the soggy sand, working his way around the dead and the dying. Exhausted by the strain, he stopped several times. Finally, after an arduous trek, he reached the foot of the flagship and called.

The Viking standing guard peered over the railing.

"By Thor's hammer," the man let out, then called others on the boat.

From the Drakkar, exhausted Vikings came to life. One laid down a plank. Two jumped over the railing to help. A huge bearded warrior slung Bodvar over his shoulder then walked up the plank.

Gwenvael followed him. "I found Ragnar too, but he is dead," he announced as he came on board.

"We will retrace your tracks in the sand and bring Ragnar back," a young Viking said then motioned to two other men. They went down the plank with a torch.

"You should take to the sea under cover of night," Gwenvael suggested to the few men aboard. "You are in no condition to face another attack."

"Vikings do not flee." The barbarian glanced at him with contempt. "We do not sail at night either... not safe."

"And this is safe?" Gwenvael laughed at the incongruity of the comment.

"We sail tonight." The labored voice came from Bodvar, who had propped himself against a rib of the hull. "Get as many good oars as you can salvage among the damaged ships. Do the same for the sails."

Gwenvael ran to support the prince ready to collapse, but Bodvar stopped him with one look.

"Collect food, water, weapons. We leave as soon as we can." Bodvar attempted to sit up straight and grunted. "Ragnar is dead." He grimaced. "No point in dying to carve him a kingdom... Later, we will avenge his death."

Gwenvael wondered about the Drakkar. It seemed to be taking on water. Would it be seaworthy?

"What about the wounded?" A tall brute asked with concern.

"Bring aboard those who can be saved. We have no room for the dying. Let the Valkyries take them to Valhalla."

Bodvar's words spread like quick fire. A flurry of stealthy activity surrounded the vessel. Under cover of the pitch black night, the Vikings loaded Ragnar's corpse and brought aboard a score of wounded.

Gwenvael wanted to tend to Bodvar's wounds, but the Viking refused his help. If he wanted to save the man's life, Gwenvael would have to remember the rudiments of the healing arts he had learned from the Ladies. Although his knowledge did not match theirs, he could recognize a good number of healing plants.

The exhausted Vikings pushed the Drakkars into deeper water, then climbed aboard and manned the oars to maneuver down the current. The flagship took the lead into the night, keeping to the middle of the river to avoid the sunken wrecks. Gwenvael counted only two other ships following them at a short distance.

In the sliver of moonlight filtering through thinning clouds, many longships protruded from the water surface at steep angles. A mast, a dragon tail, a prow, like crosses in a Christian cemetery... As the ship left the village behind, it slowed and stopped, eliciting oaths among the rowers.

"What is it?" Gwenvael could barely hide his dread.

A Viking stopped bailing and looked in Bodvar's direction. "Something dragging. Could be nets, or ropes."

"You," Bodvar ordered another with a movement of the chin. "Go see what it is, before the next ship rams us from the rear."

The designated Viking, slender compared to the others, climbed down the rope at the side of the prow.

Gwenvael could not help but admire how Bodvar still controlled his men, even wounded as he was, barely able to sit.

Moments later, the slender warrior reappeared, dripping, with a triumphant smile.

"The Britons thought fishing nets and floating hemp ropes would prevent us from passing through!" The man laughed, brandishing his knife. "Nothing a good blade cannot slice."

"Take us home," Bodvar ordered grimly.

The dip of the oars resumed. The wind had died and the rain stopped. The air smelled clean, despite traces of smoke and blood clinging to the boat. Silence fell among the survivors, disturbed only by the regular rasp of oars against the oarlocks, the gentle slapping of water against the hull, and the rhythmic scooping of the bailers.

Gwenvael considered himself lucky to have survived the carnage. So few Vikings had. Three boats out of eighty... But even these survivors may not make it to safety. *Dear God, in your infinite clemency, spare these wretched, lost souls.*

On this starless night, no one dared sail the dark sea, except for three dragonships taking on water, rowing north along the western coast of Alba.

Chapter Eleven

Through the open window of Pressine's chambers, Joyous notes rang from a distant horn.

"The king's party is approaching! Hurry." Pressine's voice lilted in anticipation as she urged the lass tying the silk sash of her deep blue gown.

Her heart raced.

"Thank you again, O mighty Goddess, for sparing my beloved," she murmured, for the hundredth time that day.

She pinched her cheeks, checked her hair in a small silver mirror, then ran out of the chamber. Breathless, she dashed up the wooden stairs leading to the top of the ramparts, to get a glimpse of Elinas.

Outside the walls, the warm afternoon sun drew steam from the fields soaked by yesterday's heavy rain. Woods and meadows, green with new growth and alive with wild flowers tossing in the breeze, seemed to rejoice in the return of their king.

The war party, still a blur at the forest line, stretched in a long ribbon, bristling with lances and colorful banners. Pressine noticed with a pang of sadness that the train scarcely reached a fraction of its numbers a month ago. The levies had probably returned to their homes, but the carnage had killed too many, and she grieved for the widows and orphans.

Although the object of her love had been spared, Pressine worried about Gwenvael. Her efforts to locate him through the water basin had failed. She dearly hoped her brother had survived. And Bodvar, was he killed? No one knew for sure. His death would place Gwenvael in great peril.

With each messenger, tales of heroic feats flew from hall to scullery and from guards to servants. The king's exploits grew to fantastic proportion with each report. Even with Caliburn, Pressine doubted that Elinas single-handedly slaughtered a whole contingent of Berserkers. Many had died bravely, to be sure, but the Britons had routed the Viking horde. Today, victory belonged to the defenders of Alba.

As the line of soldiers neared the fort, Pressine recognized Elinas, tall and proud on his dappled gray, still wearing her scarf on his left shoulder. How she had missed him.

The young man riding to the king's right, dark and slim, must be the Edling, Mattacks, returning from fosterage in Whithorn. And the prelate with a red cape on the king's left must be Bishop Renald, the boy's tutor. Pressine did not see Dewain, but the messengers said the old man had returned to Ayre to visit his son.

Behind the king's escort, eight burly men carried a wooden pallet, on which lay the life-size statue of a woman, carved in black stone. A cortege followed, and Pressine heard chanting, like in a religious procession.

When the head of the column reached the main gate, Pressine hurried down the rampart steps to meet her future husband.

The castle guards, waiting in two lines on each side of the gate, raised their spears, cheering when the riders crossed into the walled enclosure. Pressine could see Elinas searching the crowd. His beard had grown a bit, making his face longer. He looked tired.

When Pressine stepped forward, the king smiled, slid off his steed, and embraced her in an unusual public display of affection. After a heady kiss, Pressine rested her head on his shoulder.

"I missed you so much," she whispered in his ear, reveling in the scent of his leather jerkin.

He kissed her neck. "I brought back your scarf."

Yet Pressine felt uneasy. She surveyed the crowd for the source of her malaise. Two paces away stood a youth in black tunic, trews, and leather boots. Tall and dark like his father but slimmer and smooth of jaw, the Edling stared at her with a deep frown.

When Pressine met his gaze, his eyes shifted and his mouth curled down at the corners in an expression of lofty disgust. Then he crossed his fingers against evil.

With a shudder of foreboding, Pressine noticed the heavy silver cross hanging from a leather tie on his chest. A Christian, like Gwenvael. But unlike her brother, Prince Mattacks seemed of the zealous sort. He had marked her as a Pagan, and his defiant stare now reflected the contempt reserved for heathens.

The Edling did not bow when Elinas introduced Pressine. The bishop, older if not wiser, hid his distaste under a false smile. His aversion for her kind might prove more dangerous than that of the youth.

When the men carrying the statue lowered the life-size sculpture in front of Pressine, she gasped in recognition. Dear Goddess!

Mistaking her reaction, Bishop Renald smiled.

"This is a very ancient representation of the Virgin Mary. A priceless relic, really. We call Her the Black Madonna. Some travelers found Her in a cave where early Christians used to worship. I am trying to persuade our king to erect a chapel for Her in this fortress, but he evaded my pleas, leaving the decision up to you, my lady."

Pressine glanced at Elinas, who watched the exchange with a mischievous grin. How sweet of him to let her decide. Elinas winked at her. Familiar with the old gods, he knew what the statue represented.

The kind face of the sculpture, the long braided hair, and the wreath on the Madonna's head were unmistakable. She wore the shift that had become the dress of the Ladies of the Lost Isle, but her sash was a serpent. The statue's ample bosom could feed the whole land, and on Her left shoulder remained the broken claws of the raven that used to perch there.

"May I count on our future queen's gracious support in this holy endeavor?" Bishop Renald crooned.

"A chapel? Here?" What in the world could motivate a Christian bishop to build a chapel for the Great Goddess?

"Yes, a chapel." Bishop Renald's eyes shone with excited enthusiasm. "Such a testimony from the early Christians of this land deserves a fitting shrine."

Pressine relished the choice of words. A chapel would make a worthy shrine, indeed. Was it possible that the bishop had no notion of the statue's real identity?

She smiled with benevolence. "What would you say if I financed the construction myself?"

Virgin Mary, Black Madonna, or Great Goddess, it mattered not what people called Her. As long as they prayed for help, the Great Goddess would gladly grant it and spread Her bounty over the land.

"Really?" The bishop's eyes grew the size of silver crowns. "Thank you, Lady Pressine. You will be rewarded in heaven for your generous devotion."

Embarrassed by such praise, Pressine suddenly felt self conscious about her hidden motives. As a Lady of the Isle, however, she took comfort in the fact that the Goddess had come to her. What an auspicious sign, like a blessing upon her mission.

* * *

Elinas rose and paced his bedchamber. "I will not cancel my wedding to fit your religious preferences!"

Despite Dewain's warnings, Elinas had not expected such hostility from his oldest son. "Who gave you the right to question my decision?"

The tall, slender youth stood firmly, facing his father with no fear in his dark eyes. "My God gives me the strength to stand up to anyone who does not recognize His supreme power. You, father, have ignored Him for too long. You must convert, then get rid of the venomous bitch you keep within these walls."

"How dare you defy me!" Elinas glared at Mattacks, unbelieving. "I love you as much as my other sons, but religion is mainly a political tool. That is why I gave you a Christian tutor."

Mattacks averted his gaze and remained silent.

Elinas resumed pacing. "I do not condone fanatics, whatever their faith. Too many crimes are committed in the name of religion. I love Pressine with all my heart, and I do not intend to give her up just because you disapprove."

Sensing no reaction, Elinas faced the Edling again. "Is that clear?"

Mattacks breathed deeply. "If she has poisoned you so that you cannot live without her, then bed the Pagan whore, but for God's sake, do not wed her."

Elinas slammed the table with a hard fist. "You will speak of your future stepmother with the respect due to a queen!"

Realizing he was shouting, Elinas struggled to regain some control and went on in an urgent tone. "You are young, Mattacks. In time you might understand, but I shall wed Pressine as planned. And no, she has not poisoned me, nor have I bedded her. She is a virgin and so wishes to remain until our wedding night. I shall respect her decision."

"But, father, she is wicked." The Edling seemed at loss for words. "She has already won the bishop with her intrigues. All Renald talks about is the Black Madonna's chapel. He has already picked a spot near the great hall and started drawing on parchment."

"Yes, Pressine has quite winsome ways. I could not have wished for a more accomplished bride." Elinas chuckled. "In the blink of an eye, she gave the bishop what he wants the most. She just turned a potential enemy into an ally who owes her a great deal. The woman is a gem."

Mattacks shook his head in plain disgust. "On your wedding night, the nuptial witnesses will find on her the mark of Satan. Remember my words."

"Very unlikely." Elinas would never subject Pressine to such a humiliating custom.

Mattacks drew breath to protest again.

Elinas raised his hand to stop him. "Since my succession is secure, no one will gawk at my naked wife but me."

"You will regret it, father."

"It is not your concern." Elinas sighed heavily, then considered his Edling with reproach. "From now on, I expect you to treat Pressine with the respect due to her rank. Whether in the hall or at the hunt, I shall tolerate no less from you. Is that understood?"

Mattacks calmly gazed into his father's eyes. "As you wish."

The Edling's neutral voice and composed face gave no clue as to his true emotions.

* * *

Pressine noticed that neither the Edling nor the Bishop attended the evening meal, but no one seemed to mind. After supper, she lingered in the hall, sitting by Elinas, holding hands under the table while listening to the generals and barons retelling stories of the great battle. She asked about strategy and inquired about the Viking's way of life. Mostly, she listened, each word bringing forth terrifying images of the bloody battle.

Then, one at a time, the candles started dying.

Elinas smiled and squeezed her hand. "Although I treasure your company, dear lady, my weary bones long for a comfortable bed."

"I understand, my lord." Pressine rose from the table. "Besides, the hunt leaves at dawn."

"I cannot believe my Edling is seventeen. I was married at that age." Elinas offered his arm. "On his first hunt as an adult he is expected to prove himself by killing some big game."

Pressine accepted the king's arm and they walked across the hall. She never cared for brutal sports, but the traditional hunt was a social event. It also had the added purpose of keeping the guests fed.

They crossed the castle yard in the balmy spring night, fragrant with lilac blossoms. When they reached the door to Pressine's chambers, the king bent for a kiss. She let herself be transported by his passion, safe in the knowledge that Elinas loved her.

He released her gently.

"Twelve days..." she whispered in his ear.

Elinas chuckled. "I have often imagined our wedding night. Perhaps the thought helped me survive, just for you."

After kissing her hand, Elinas walked away toward his chambers across the courtyard. Pressine watched him go. When he glanced back and waved, her heart jumped and she blew him a kiss. *Thank you, Dear Goddess, for keeping him alive!*

* * *

When Elinas knocked on her door before dawn, Pressine had already dressed. Together, they walked through the sleepy castle grounds, to the stables. There, the hunting party gathered in a frenzy of hooves, creaking saddles and deerhound barks.

Pressine let go of the king's hand to allow him to greet his barons in a dignified manner. The horses whinnied and fidgeted. Servants and guards ran among beasts and riders, carrying torches, crossbows and spears. A lad brought Pressine's white mare.

"Let me help you," Elinas said softly. Seizing her by the waist, he lifted her into the saddle.

Heat rose to her cheeks when his strong hand held her aloft, then gently deposited her on the horse, lingering on her thigh while he checked the leather straps. Pressine brushed his knuckles with gloved fingers. Glancing up, the king took her hand to his lips.

Across from Pressine, among the hunters, the Edling mounted a skittish black stallion who excited the mares. She caught Mattacks' flicker of condemnation as their eyes met. With a proud shake of the head, the young man threw back his long dark hair. He looked too serious, too conceited for seventeen, as if he already carried the weight of his father's crown.

Conan, the second son, as fair as the elder was dark, had been allowed to follow the hunt as an observer. Pressine, however, noticed the unobtrusive sling hanging from his belt. The younger prince seemed eager to please, watching his father's every move. Struggling for control over a huge bay, the boy gave Pressine a timid smile.

When the sky paled in the east, Elinas sounded his silver horn. Lining up behind him, the hunters followed their king and future queen through the main gate onto the forest road. A pinkish dawn prompted the larks to sing when the party entered the canopy of trees. Pressine filled her lungs with the green earthy smell of the undergrowth. In the wan light, morning dew twinkled on grasses and leaves.

Apart from weapons and hounds, the hunt resembled a pleasant ride in the woods, until Pressine caught sight of a boar. The black creature bolted out of a thicket and crossed the path, unsettling the horses. Judging by the many scars on its hide, the old solitary beast with sharp yellow tusks must have survived many skirmishes.

"The boar is mine!" Young Mattacks spurred his stallion ahead to chase the prey.

Mattacks' stallion reared. An accomplished rider, the Edling remained on his mount. The boar had stopped to face the young prince.

Elinas nudged his steed protectively in front of Pressine's mare. The hound master strained against the pull of the hounds, barking and ready to tear the prey to pieces.

"Hold the dogs!" Mattacks shouted.

The boar charged. Mattacks thrust his spear. The blade stabbed but the handle broke. The Edling lost his balance and fell to the ground. The squealing prey fled through the trees, the spear blade jutting out of its leathery back.

Leaping upon the stallion like an acrobat, Mattacks went after the beast, leaving the other hunters to follow the hoof prints and blood trail in the wake of the sniffing dogs.

Pressine turned around. Behind her, Conan had gone pale. The lad knew how dangerous a wounded beast could be. *If his brother dies, he is the next in line*, she thought almost wistfully. Ashamed of thinking such ill, Pressine reminded herself that the Goddess would handle things Her own way.

* * *

Ducking under low branches, Mattacks pursued his prey. Twigs snapped and saplings whipped his arms as the stallion galloped through the brush. It was his hunt. He would bring down the boar and force the respect of all the soft bellied barons his father called councilors.

Even Bishop Renald had betrayed him by siding with the Pagan bitch. Now, Mattacks stood alone in the shadow of God and, strong in his untainted faith, he would prevail.

Mattacks had waited long enough, studied long enough. His time had come, and he would show his father what sort of mettle the future king was made of. For Mattacks would be king. And unlike his father softened by age, he would rule with an iron grip, feared and respected throughout the land.

No one would stand against him unpunished, and certainly not a filthy heathen. The clergy had grown soft in Strathclyde. A strong Christian king could reinstate confiscations, and floggings for doing the devil's work.

But a heathen priestess deserved to burn alive.

The boar weakened and slowed its pace. Mattacks had almost caught up with it when the wounded beast faced about and grunted, lowering its head. The warm stench of the swine spread through the clearing.

Dismounting, Mattacks faced the ferocious tusks and drew his hunting knife, heart pounding, poised to face the charge. With the hunt far behind, he stood alone. *In God's shadow,* he reminded himself, taking heart in His mighty protection.

Mattacks stood his ground when the boar charged. At the last possible moment, he leapt to the side, avoiding the razor-sharp tusks. The blade missed the mark, only slashing the hide. Fortunately, he hung on to the knife. Running to the other side of the clearing, he waited for the next charge.

Blood oozing from its wounds, the black beast slowly turned around. Its small eyes under grimy lashes never wandered, but stared straight into Mattacks' own.

Sure of himself, Mattacks glared back at the beast. With practiced agility, he moved from side to side to confuse the prey. When Mattacks stopped in front of a small tree and goaded the animal, exhorting it to fight, the boar charged again. Mattacks jumped clear, leaving the beast to slam into the tree and bury its tusks in the tender pulp.

While the beast heaved to pull free of the trunk, Mattacks thrust his sharp blade to the hilt below the jowl, then sliced through the throat, cutting short the frantic squeals.

"Die, you filthy spawn of Satan," he muttered, thinking of other filth he would like to slash open. Around him, hot blood spurted and pooled deep red, before seeping through the bed of dead leaves into the spongy ground. The boar collapsed. Thrashing in the throes of death, it gurgled a last breath.

The hunting party arrived just in time to witness the triumph. Aware of the dogs howling madly at the smell of fresh blood, Mattacks cleaned his blade on the hide and rose. Wiping bloody hands on his trews, he faced his father. After a slight bow to the king, hiding his jubilation, Mattacks signaled the servants, winded from running behind the horses.

"Take it away," he ordered with feigned indifference.

Inside, however, he exulted. If God gave him the strength to do this, with God's help, Mattacks could do anything... Including eradicate paganism from his future kingdom.

* * *

That night, Pressine joined the feast in the hall. Sitting at the high table with Elinas, she watched Mattacks at a side table with the hunters and other young nobles. He received all the attention due a hero, telling and retelling the story of his kill with feigned boredom.

Well into the banquet, Elinas nodded to Pressine and let go of her hand. He rose and tapped his dirk on the silver cup he shared with her.

The guests quieted.

"Tonight, we count one more valiant man in our ranks," Elinas declared, full of fatherly pride. "The Edling proved his courage in the hunt, if not yet in battle."

The king picked up his family sword from the back of his chair, then called his son to the high table.

If Mattacks was surprised, he did not show it as he ambled confidently to his father's side.

Elinas handed his son the heirloom. "My son, please accept this token of valor. May you always make me proud as you did today."

With an unreadable smile, Mattacks accepted the family sword and bowed slightly.

Elinas filled his cup with mead and handed it to Mattacks with a flourish. "After drinking this, you can choose any servant girl you like for the night."

The guests cheered and raised their cups.

The Edling held up one hand, asking for silence. "I do not indulge in such libations, nor do I fornicate like a heathen."

A general gasp answered.

"His Holiness the Pope recently condemned such practices, and I pray no one commits these sins in my presence," he said with open disdain.

As the Edling returned to his table, Bishop Renald gave a thin smile of approval, but the comment brought a wave of muffled protests from the hunters.

Unruffled, Elinas smiled at Pressine. He did not seem to notice the uneasy silence that ensued, but Pressine did. Soon, the servants brought the next course, and the conversations resumed.

Seized by foreboding, Pressine could not share in the general cheer. The intransigence and the calculating coldness of the Edling chilled her to the marrow.

Chapter Twelve

On the tenth day after the Viking defeat in Alba, a single Drakkar sailed into view of Arstinchar. A score of starving survivors cluttered the deck, some wounded. At the aft, rolled into a sail, lay the stinking corpse of Prince Ragnar. The two other longships that escaped after the battle had vanished during a night storm days ago.

Gwenvael wondered at the wisdom of returning to the Viking stronghold. Bodvar drifted in and out of consciousness, sometimes lucid, sometimes feverish. If by misfortune he died, Gwenvael could very well become a slave himself. *Dear God, do not let this happen!*

Staring in surprise beyond the circle of half-sunken palisades protecting the Viking harbor, Gwenvael saw a great fleet. Feathered banners, leather ribbons, bones, and fur ornaments floated atop a myriad masts.

"New arrivals from Gotland," the red-headed giant named Olaf volunteered with a smile as they crossed into the enclave.

How many more warriors would pour on the shores of Alba? Even with the Ladies' help, how long could the Britons fend them off? It seemed a losing battle. *God Almighty, please protect my countrymen.*

The Drakkar came to shore among loud cheers. Did these people know they had lost the battle?

Four Vikings carried Bodvar off the ship on a pallet of shields and oars, and took him to his longhouse. After lowering him through the small entrance, they laid him on the wooden platform of the central room.

Bodvar shook feverishly, delirious, moaning in pain. Gwenvael had no way of telling whether he had improved or worsened. The Viking's life rested in the hands of God.

Cliona emerged from her room. At the sight of her troubled face and teary emerald eyes, Gwenvael realized he had come home. When had he started thinking of Arstinchar as home? He could not say, but it had much to do with Cliona. Wherever she resided felt like home.

She threw herself into his arms. Her fiery hair smelled like a field of flowers in summer.

"I thought I might never see you again." Gwenvael kissed her throat with the passion he had kept in check since he had left her.

When she stiffened slightly in his embrace, a realization struck him.

"Have they forced you?" As he caressed her hair, he knew.

Cliona sobbed on his chest, tears rolling down her cheeks.

"When the new horde came," she explained between sobs, "they demanded sexual favors. A slave must submit or die. And I wanted to live to see you again."

Gwenvael understood only too well and felt guilty at not having freed Cliona earlier. He held her protectively against him. "It will never happen again. I promise. As soon as Bodvar recovers, I shall ask for your freedom." *If he recovers...* But if he did survive, how could he refuse his savior anything?

Cliona's eyes gleamed through the tears.

Gwenvael hesitated before asking, "Would you be my wife?"

A glorious smile brightened Cliona's face. "You would do this for me?"

"Yes, and much more." He brushed her lips in a tender kiss.

Olaf's entrance broke the happy reunion. "We need you to help with the preparations for Ragnar's funeral."

Clearing his throat, Gwenvael detached himself from Cliona. "I just need a moment."

While Olaf stood, waiting, Gwenvael checked Bodvar's bandages and tightened his shoulder brace made of armor plates.

"I still cannot believe you shoved that shoulder back in place." Olaf grinned. "I thought the warriors on the boat would throw you overboard for making our prince scream like a bairn."

"Sometimes the treatment is painful, but the results are worth it." Satisfied, Gwenvael followed Olaf outside.

As they walked toward the beach, news of the brutal defeat and loss of so many warriors, far from sapping the Vikings' morale, became an excuse for celebration.

"Death in battle is something to rejoice about," Olaf explained. "It secures passage into Valhalla."

Gwenvael assumed it was the Viking's heaven. As they reached the beach, the survivors from the battle were digging a pit in the sand. Nearby, Ragnar's corpse, still rolled in the sail, vilified the air and attracted seagulls.

Accepting a shovel, Gwenvael dug with the others. Then the warriors sat Ragnar's corpse at the bottom of the hole and placed a drinking horn in his hand. In front of him, on a segment of tree trunk, they laid fruit and a pitcher of mead. Then they covered the hole with planks.

Gwenvael frowned. "Is that how you bury the dead?"

Olaf smiled. "We leave him to eat and drink merrily until his funeral. He will travel to Valhalla on a longship named Nagelfar, after the ship that carries glorious dead warriors to Ragnarok, the final battle of the gods."

"When will that be?" Gwenvael worried about the stench.

Olaf swatted at a fly. "Since he has been dead ten days already, we can have the ceremony very soon."

Gwenvael did not understand the relevance. "Why not take care of the dead right away?"

"When the great god Odin died, he came back to life after nine days. So, we always wait ten... just to be sure." Olaf chuckled. "And then the living have to feast and drink, too."

Nodding, Gwenvael remembered his precarious status in Arstinchar. "Since Bodvar is wounded, who is in charge?"

"Sigurd is the leader of the new fleet. He wants to see us all in the chieftain's hall."

"Me, too?" Gwenvael shuddered with foreboding.

"Of course. You are part of the survivors." Olaf smiled. "Besides, you live in Bodvar's house. You represent him until he can attend in person."

Later, in the hall, members of the most prominent houses stood in front of Sigurd, who sat in the high chair. Despite his fair grasp of the language, Gwenvael did not quite understand the subtleties of the lengthy deliberations. But he realized that a prince's funeral was a major ceremony. The preparations would cost much in gold, animals, lumber and craftsmanship, as well as in fine cloth and women's labor.

Finally, Sigurd called before him the four young women of Ragnar's household. They stood very still, staring back in deadly silence. At first, Gwenvael believed them stunned by the shock of their lord's demise.

"Which of you claims the privilege of accompanying her prince on his last voyage?" Sigurd's solemn face and tone spoke of ancient rituals and ancestral customs.

Gwenvael wondered at the question.

None of the women volunteered.

"You!" Sigurd designated the youngest and prettiest of the lot, a blonde beauty with delicate features.

The girl's eyes widened and she gasped.

"What is your name?" Sigurd asked in the same ceremonial manner.

Open fear washed over the young woman's face. She could not be more than sixteen, and her small breasts heaved as she glanced around. She reminded Gwenvael of a hare caught in a snare. Finally, in the oppressive silence, under the stares of the assembled men, she composed her face.

"My name is Asa, my lord," she said in a barely audible voice.

"Do not be afraid, Asa," Sigurd offered in a softer tone. "The Valkyries will carry you to Valhalla with your lover, and you will share his glory and be spared the petty sufferings of this life."

Trembling, Asa bowed. "I am honored to be chosen."

No wonder the girl shook. What barbaric custom would sacrifice such a pure young woman? And for what? A dead tyrant? By bringing Christian notions to these savages, Gwenvael hoped to change all that. But now was not the time.

"Go and be merry, Asa." Sigurd indulged her with a paternal smile. "From now on, you can have anything you want. Every person in Arstinchar will yield to your slightest whim."

Asa filed out of the hall with the other women, two sturdy warriors following them closely. What a pity! Gwenvael guessed the lass would not be left alone for an instant until the sacrifice. No hope of escape for her.

Gwenvael remembered to breathe.

From then on, the whole population of Arstinchar, over three thousand people, worked feverishly for the ceremony. By night, they ate and drank heavily. The survivors dragged on dry sand the chosen longboat for the funeral, the Nagelfar. It would become Ragnar's last residence. Warriors fitted the Drakkar for the funeral while, the women sewed luxurious clothes to send the prince and his consort to Valhalla in the most fitting finery.

A filthy crone in stinking rags they called the Angel of Death, supervised all the ceremonial details. As much as he tried, Gwenvael could find in her weathered face, lanky hair, and twisted body, no resemblance to the Christian Angel of Death, Michael. It felt sacrilegious to honor this old harpy as highly as the glorious Archangel who would lead the souls chosen by God into eternal light after Judgment Day.

The crone, however, must have had some healing knowledge. When she visited Bodvar, she inspected his armor shell with interest and nodded her approval. "You should use spider webs in your poultice."

Gwenvael could not hide his surprise. "I never heard of that."

"It works, but I do not have any on me. You will have to collect them yourself." The old woman pulled small pebbles out of a leather pouch at her belt and threw them in the air.

Gwenvael had heard about such ways of divination but had never seen it done before. The Angel of Death squatted to study the position of the pebbles on the earthen floor. Reading the runes carved upon them, she shrugged.

"He shall live and fight again," she declared, then retrieved the pebbles and left the house without a backward glance.

With Cliona's help, Gwenvael treated Bodvar with herbal brews and poultices. Upon her insistence, he also used the spider webs recommended by the crone. The strange treatment worked. Within two days the fever abated. To Gwenvael's delight, Bodvar ate voraciously. As his strength returned, he started to walk again, strolling about Arstinchar, left arm tightly bound to his chest.

"Did you warn the Britons about our raid?" he asked Gwenvael, as he inspected a new battle axe, under the lean-to that served as a forge.

"No, I did not." Gwenvael's heart beat faster as he raised his voice over the hammering of the blacksmith. "How could I? I did not even know when or where you planned to attack."

"True. No one did. So, how could they have set an ambush?" Bodvar swung the axe, dangerously close to Gwenvael's head.

Gwenvael took a step back, and glanced at the sweaty blacksmith, who elicited sparks from incandescent metal. "The Ladies have the sight."

Bodvar grunted. "You really believe that?"

"I have seen it with my own eyes." How much could Gwenvael tell? The place smelled of molten metal, hot as hell itself. Let the truth set him free. "My sister scries in a water basin to bring forth visions of what is to come."

"Does she?" Bodvar stared at Gwenvael as if to determine whether or not he was lying. "Then I believe you. Besides, if you had betrayed me, why would you save my life and return here?"

"Why indeed?" Gwenvael wondered at that himself.

Bodvar set the axe back on the work bench. "Of course, you sent me to the trap of the Lost Isle, then rescued me from drowning. Why?"

Gwenvael scrambled for a truthful answer. "I believe it was God's will, because we must do His work together."

Reaching for a sword on a rack, Bodvar shook his head. "I do not want to hear another word about your stupid god."

Searching for a new topic, Gwenvael remembered his promise to Cliona. "I have a favor to ask."

Running his fingers along the edge of the sword blade, Bodvar cocked an eyebrow. "Well, what is it?"

"Something about Cliona."

"Oh!" Bodvar stopped to stare at Gwenvael. "You do not like her anymore? You want another slave? You Briton rascal!" He smiled and slapped Gwenvael's thigh with the flat of the blade.

"Not at all!" Gwenvael rubbed his smarting thigh. "I want to marry her. I want her to be free."

Bodvar's face grew serious. Slowly, he set the sword back on its rack. "In Odin's name, what for? A slave is easier to control and far more eager to please."

"I love her." Gwenvael sustained the Viking's gaze, hoping the man would understand.

"Love? Bah!" Bodvar suddenly turned away, fending off a fly with a wave of the hand, and walked out of the forge.

Gwenvael would not be dismissed so easily and ran after him. "Love is what my God teaches."

"Love makes men silly." Bodvar marched ahead in long strides. "We have mead for that."

"But a man in love cannot help himself. Just like with mead."

Bodvar chuckled and turned about. "You are an odd fellow. But what you are asking goes against my people's rules."

"All great leaders change the rules for the better." Would brazen flattery work on Bodvar?

The Viking grunted. "Only because you saved my life again, I will present your request to the council. But I doubt they will agree."

Chapter Thirteen

At the sound of the horn, Pressine dropped the golden wedding gown into Ceinwyn's lap and ran to the open window. Could it be?

A soldier hurried across the courtyard toward her chambers. She motioned to him.

The man came to the open window and bowed. "Lady Pressine! Your guest approaches the gate!"

"Ceinwyn, come!" Pressine rushed out into the bright afternoon sun bathing the yard.

Light as a fluttering bird, she flew past the great hall on her way to the main gate, and arrived just in time to see Morgane and her retinue riding through the stone arch. In a blue shift, Lady Morgane rode side-saddle, head high, a raven perched on her shoulder. As she halted her mare, a crowd of servants and visitors quickly formed around her party. In her wake, young servants on ponies came to a halt, while children on foot prodded the pack animals with sticks.

Pressine waved and ran toward her aunt. "Morgane! Ogyr! I am so glad to see both of you."

Ogyr cawed a greeting and flew to Pressine's shoulder.

Pressine laughed, caressing the bird's head gently, and kissed its feathery wing. "Hello to you, Old Friend. I thought I told you to stay with Gwenvael."

"I understand Ogyr does not care for the Vikings." Morgane chuckled. "Something about boiling in a pot. So he returned to the safety of the Lost Isle."

Pressine remembered the army of barbarians from the visions. "Can you blame him?"

She reached up to help Morgane dismount. Morgane took her hand and slid down the mare. As they embraced, Pressine delighted in the lavender scent of her aunt's braided hair. Briefly, she longed for the peace of the small island, but her place was here. On her shoulder, Ogyr spread his wings for balance.

"Come." Pressine took Morgane by the hand. "Let the servants take the trunks to your chambers. There is something I want to show you."

The servants took away the animals and the traveling chests, and the curious dispersed.

"Where is Elinas?" Morgane glanced around with interest. "And what about this Mattacks, the heir you told me about?"

Pressine motioned with her chin in the direction of the stables. "Over there. It's the Edling talking with Bishop Renald. The two crows, I call them. Both wearing black, strutting straight as spears. They are inseparable."

Morgane squinted at the two men in the distance. "And the king? I have not seen him since he was a child."

"With his councilors. He will be in the hall for the evening meal." Pressine stopped walking and stared at her aunt. "You radiate health and happiness!"

"It is the child growing inside me." Morgane patted her still flat belly. "A healthy boy, just as I wished."

"A boy?" Surprised, Pressine shivered at the implications. The Ladies rarely fared well with male children. Her mother almost died giving birth to Gwenvael. "What if he is deformed?"

"We cannot stop having babies for fear of a male child." Morgane exuded confidence. "If the Goddess wishes a boy, she will watch over him."

Unconvinced, Pressine resumed walking toward the great hall and changed the topic. "I am glad you saw Bodvar escape the battle alive with Gwenvael in your visions."

Morgane pressed her lips. "But I fear that new Viking Horde in Arstinchar."

"Nothing is ever perfect." Pressine exhaled slowly, to erase the new threat from her mind and focus on this happy moment. "It is so good to see you, smell you. I missed your sound advice."

"Any problems with the wedding?" Morgane slowed her pace and glanced at her with a coy smile.

"I fear for my sanity." An understatement. "The bishop insists on a high mass."

Morgane frowned. "And the king?"

"Elinas will defer to my wishes, but judging by his choice at our betrothal, he would prefer a druidic ceremony. All I want is the blessing of the Goddess." Pressine sighed. "This is all so confusing."

Morgane's smoky eyes looked perplexed for a moment then sparkled with life. "Why not have all three? Three is a sacred number in every religion. Your groom is king after all. Too much blessing cannot hurt. That way everyone is happy."

"I knew you would come up with a solution." Without missing a step, Pressine glanced at the two men in black coming her way and lowered her voice. "I doubt the bishop will approve."

Taking Pressine's hint, Morgane whispered. "You could argue that since the people of this country observe different faiths, you must acknowledge them all in order to rally their support."

"It makes good sense." Pressine wondered why she hadn't thought of it. "Elinas will love this idea."

Morgane stopped short in front of the statue standing on a pedestal by the entrance of the great hall.

Pressine chuckled. "Here is the surprise."

"Mighty Goddess! Where did you find this?"

"I found it in a cave." Bishop Renald, who'd hurried to catch up with the two women, answered for Pressine. He sounded out of breath but beamed with pride. "A Black Madonna, one of the oldest statues of the Virgin Mary worshiped by the early Christians of Whithorn."

"Indeed!" Morgane's face reflected genuine interest.

"Bishop Renald, at your service, my lady." The bishop bowed. "You must be Lady Morgane, our future queen's aunt. I can see the family resemblance."

Morgane curtsied.

"And this is Prince Mattacks," Pressine said, as the Edling joined them somewhat reluctantly.

Mattacks smiled with disdain and did not bow.

Morgane raised a brow but did not remark on his rudeness.

Bristling at Mattacks' attitude, Pressine hid her anger. "The Lord Bishop asked me to build a chapel to shelter his rare find, and I accepted."

"I see..." A playful spark lit Morgane's gray eyes.

Enjoying Morgane's mirth, Pressine pointed to a pile of stones to the side of the Great Hall. "The construction just started. When it is completed, pilgrims from all over the land will come to worship this symbol of pure grace and motherly love."

"What a wonderful idea!" Morgane smiled to the bishop. "I shall come and worship myself every time I pass this way."

Pressine caught Mattacks' harsh look of hatred directed at the two women. As dark and handsome as Elinas, he lacked his father's compassion.

Morgane turned her back to the prince and took the bishop by the arm. "Tell me, Lord Bishop, why does the Black Madonna use a serpent for a sash?"

The bishop spoke like a kind teacher. "Mary is universal love incarnate, you see... Her absolute purity allows her to forgive even the snake for the damning of Adam and Eve."

"Really?" Morgane indicated the broken claws on the statue's shoulder. "And why would she carry a raven, like my niece here?"

Although Pressine enjoyed seeing the bishop cringe, she wished Morgane would stop her allusions. The man was dense but might catch on if he knew anything at all about the old faith.

Renald seemed annoyed but smiled nevertheless. "I believe the missing bird must have been a dove, the Christian symbol of peace and love."

Morgane grinned. "And why would they use black stone?"

The bishop fingered his rosary one notch, and his smile grew strained. "The early Christians knew that Mary was born in the east Mediterranean lands, where the hot sun gives people darker skin. Some races in the south even have black skin, or so I understand. These early worshipers probably assumed that Mary had dark skin as well."

"Like the legendary folks of our land." Morgane seemed deep in thought. "Then you believe Mary did not have dark skin, and her son was fair, right?"

"Quite right. Blond and blue-eyed Our Savior was." The bishop's fingers moved faster on the rosary. "And it is not our place to question the scriptures, Lady Morgane, but to worship the one true God."

Morgane smiled benignly. "How convenient."

Morgane, stop!

Mattacks tensed and pressed his lips together, as if to suppress a caustic comment.

The bishop shuffled his feet and flashed an embarrassed smile. "I know you would like to get settled in as soon as possible. So, I shall not stand in your way. We can resume this conversation another time."

Bishop Renald lifted his black hat and left, followed by Mattacks.

"This way." Pressine led Morgane in the opposite direction.

"The heir did not say a single word," Morgane remarked, as soon as they had walked out of earshot. "He shows too much restraint for one so young."

Pressine nodded. "He entertained murderous thoughts. I could see the tension in his face."

"As could I." Suddenly, Morgane rolled her eyes and exploded in uncontrollable laughter. "A black Madonna, the Virgin Mary! Indeed! The Goddess works in mysterious ways!"

Pressine joined in the gaiety. "Come see your chambers."

"Yes, I need a bath," Morgane said cheerfully. "And I want to meet that apprentice of yours. Ceinwyn, is it?"

"Yes, Ceinwyn."

* * *

Walking through the compound, deep in thought, Mattacks rehearsed his plan. He would not have a heathen for stepmother and another for great aunt. He must find a way to stop the wedding.

He found his brother Conan at the kennel, as he knew he would. The silly youth loved the hounds as much as their father did. As if soulless animals should matter to a king!

Mattacks wrinkled his nose. "What a foul-smelling place, full of howls and barks, straight from hell."

Grinning, Conan glanced up from the greyhound he was combing. "Hounds are good company."

Mattacks approached the lad with an engaging smile. "So, little brother, how do you feel about our father getting married?"

Conan shrugged. "I think Father deserves to be happy."

"And what of the bride?" Had the nitwit any opinion at all?

The boy plucked a tick from the dog's pelt and squashed it between two thumbnails, then scratched the animal behind the ears. "Pressine is kind and young, and pretty...and smart too. He could have chosen much worse."

Mattacks dropped on one knee to his brother's level. "You like her then?"

"Of course, I like her. Who would not?" Conan stood up and threw a stick.

The dog darted after it.

Conan's blue eyes narrowed. "Why? You don't like her?"

Mattacks rose, dusting his black trews. "Does it not bother you that she will replace our mother in the king's heart and in his bed? Can you imagine them fornicating like hounds?"

"I never thought of that." Conan blushed pink and lowered his gaze. "But as long as they are married, there is nothing wrong with that, is it?"

"Nothing wrong?" Mattacks tried to sound horrified. "What if they have children?"

Conan pushed a blond strand of hair away from his face. "Then I guess we shall have more brothers and sisters."

"Right." Mattacks could not help a sneer. "And the brats will murder us for our inheritance."

"Your inheritance, brother." Conan stared straight into Mattacks' eyes. "Not mine."

"Could be yours if I died." Mattacks looked away. His brother was too dumb to get such ideas. "But you are still a child. You do not understand the gravity of the situation."

"I am thirteen," Conan protested, full of challenge. "Not a child anymore."

"Oh? So where is your sword? I only see a sling at your belt, and I wager you never killed anything with it."

"I did, too."

Mattacks pulled out his dirk with a flourish. "Now, this is a man's blade. It killed a wild boar. I bet you this dagger that you cannot shoot a raven at twenty paces."

Conan glanced at the ornate weapon suspiciously. "I can do it."

"Well, there is a raven in the oak near the stables. I bet you cannot hit the dumb bird."

"I will prove you wrong."

Mattacks pulled meat scraps from his pocket. "We can bait the bird with those, but I do not believe you can kill it."

Conan resolutely started toward the oak.

Walking beside his brother, Mattacks smiled inwardly. How easily he could manipulate the weak. Observation, diplomacy, strength of character, these were the primary virtues of a ruler, and he possessed them all. He would make a fine king someday. And it would happen soon if his father behaved foolishly, and let evil women poison his mind. Mattacks could have the king declared unfit by the council.

Mattacks set the scraps on the stone bench under the oak, then the two brothers hid behind the hazelnut bush and waited silently. Soon, the raven flew down from his branch and pecked at the bait.

Mattacks remained very quiet as he watched Conan fit a rock in the leather sling. There could be only one throw. If the boy missed, he would not get another chance.

The sling gyrated through the air with a faint whirr. When Conan let fly, the stone hurled faster than a bolt. The rock impacted with a soft thud, knocking the bird off the bench. The raven flopped to the ground, inert.

Mattacks applauded. "Good shot, Brother. I am very impressed. I never thought you were that good," he lied.

"Told you!" Conan beamed with naive pride.

Mattacks laid one hand on Conan's shoulder and offered him the dirk, hilt first. "Here is your prize, Brother. You earned it. May I keep the bird?"

Taking the blade, Conan shrugged. "If you want to, but carrion is no good to eat."

"I know. I would like to have it stuffed, as a souvenir."

Sliding dirk and sling into his belt, Conan grinned, obviously reveling in his victory. Mattacks answered the smile in kind, but his thoughts traveled along a different path.

* * *

The next morning, when Pressine opened the shutters, something knocked and bounced off the wooden slats.

She screamed.

Hanging from a string tied to the eaves, a raven swayed upside down in the morning breeze. It was Ogyr, and he was dead.

"What is it, my lady?" Ceinwyn rushed to Pressine's side. "Who on earth?" Hastily, the girl closed the shutters.

Pressine slowed her breathing, trying to calm the beating of her heart. Horror and grief yielded to anger. "I think I know who did this and why." She walked away from the window.

"Who would do such a thing?"

"Sorry, Ceinwyn, I cannot tell you. Not until I am certain." She snatched her robe from the foot of the bed.

"But if you know who did this, you should tell the king, my lady," Ceinwyn said with vehemence. "Such cruelty should not go unpunished."

"I agree." Sadness and anger battled in Pressine's mind, but she must remain strong.

Pressine could not tell anyone whom she suspected, not even Ceinwyn, and certainly not Elinas. One did not accuse the Edling on a hunch without irrefutable proof. Who would believe that such a refined, handsome, exemplary religious man, a future king, could be so hateful? Pressine, however, could sense the devious mind under the polished surface.

"Go tell Morgane," she ordered Ceinwyn.

As soon as the lass had gone, Pressine ran through the courtyard that separated her chambers from those of the king and knocked on the heavy door.

A sleepy page with tousled hair opened it and bowed at the sight of her. "My lady... I shall tell the king you have come."

"Do not bother, child. I can introduce myself." Pressine crossed the antechamber.

"But, my lady," the page protested, following her.

"Let me through." After a soft knock, Pressine pushed open the door to the king's bedchamber.

Sitting on the bed, Elinas looked up, delighted surprise on his face. Quickly, he cinched the waist strings of his trews, rose, then raked long fingers through his thick dark hair as he came to meet her. "Pressine, what prompted such an early visit?"

Suddenly self-conscious about her own neglected appearance, Pressine groped for words. "Sorry to startle you, My Lord, but... someone in these walls killed my pet raven, Ogyr, and hung its carcass in front of my bedroom window."

"What?" The king's face went from pale to red under the black stubby beard. "Who would have the perverse audacity to offend my chosen queen?"

Coming to Pressine, he took her in his arms. "Are you all right?"

"I will be fine." She forced a smile as he kissed her forehead lightly. How could she possibly tell him she suspected Mattacks? "I only have vague suspicions, my lord, so I refuse to make accusations. But I would like to inquire into the matter, with your permission, of course."

"Yes, dearest lady. But please be discreet." Elinas cleared his throat. "With all the guests arriving every day, I do not want to start false rumors and spoil our wedding. I shall have someone question the servants."

Fear suddenly gripped Pressine and she separated herself from the king's embrace. "I wonder whether we should postpone the wedding until this matter is settled. Such a hateful display feels like a warning."

"I shall not yield to intimidation in my own fortress. The wedding will go as planned." Elinas broke into a smile. "By the way, the idea of three ceremonies is the best strategy I have heard in a long time. I like your aunt Morgane. How much older than you is she? I thought I remembered seeing her once, when I was still a child, but she cannot be that old."

"She is older than she looks, my lord." Pressine could not reveal the Ladies' longevity, not yet. After the wedding, there would be ample time to explain. "Aunt Morgane would never forgive me for divulging her age."

Elinas offered Pressine a chair. "I will never ask again. Perhaps it was someone who looked like her."

"Perhaps." Pressine sat at the table and smiled, but she wondered how Elinas would take the news that she, like her aunt, would never age.

"In any case, I am glad she came." Elinas pulled a chair and sat across the table. "I have a surprise arriving for you today."

"A gift?" Pressine's heart raced at her king's kindness.

Elinas paused mysteriously. "A troupe of minstrels from Bretagne. They will perform at the feast."

"How wondrous!" Pressine's excitement rose. "Where did you find them?"

"In Whithorn, where they entertained King Emrys of Galloway. They will make our wedding an unforgettable event for all our guests as well." Elinas took her hand across the table and kissed her fingers.

"Thank you, my lord, for such kindness." Suddenly Pressine thought of home. "It has been so long since I heard from Bretagne. Sometimes it feels like a dream, or another life. Does my native land still exist, somewhere beyond the sea? It seems so far away."

Elinas brought her close over the table, as if for a kiss.

Young voices argued in the antechamber. Pressine glanced toward the door as Conan irrupted into the room. The kiss would have to wait.

Elinas let go of Pressine's hands and sat far back into his chair. "What happened to your manners, son. How dare you barge in here unannounced?"

Pressine smiled flirtatiously. "You did not scold me that way, my lord."

Elinas stared grimly at young Conan. "I hope you have a good reason for disturbing our conversation."

Gravely, the lad came to kneel in front of his father. "I just learned about Lady Pressine's raven. I am the one who killed the bird yesterday."

Pressine gasped, astounded. "But why?"

Conan looked up at her with a contrite face. "I did not know the raven was yours, my lady. I give you my word."

At a loss for words, Pressine struggled to understand but could not. Why would sweet Conan kill her magic bird?

Turning to Elinas, the boy added, "I killed it under the oak, to show off my skills with the sling. I did not know... honestly!"

"Did you also hang the carcass in front of Lady Pressine's window?" Elinas sounded threatening.

"Certainly not!" Conan rose in protest. "Why would I do such a vile thing?"

Vile indeed. Pressine could not suppress her tears and had to look away.

"Then, who did?" the king asked in a steely voice.

"I could not say, Father. I did not see it done."

"But surely you have some idea of who it was." The king's chilly tone demanded an answer.

"Expect nothing more from me, Father. I am ready to take whatever punishment you see fit. That is all I can do."

"I appreciate your honesty, son, but this prank has gone too far. Whose idea was this? Who hung up the raven?"

Conan stared at the flagstone and remained silent. Was the lad protecting his older brother? Did he want to spare his father the painful truth?

"At least the deed was not premeditated," Elinas concluded. "So it could not be a warning. There is no reason for alarm. Some scullion must have found the bird and played a stupid prank. And I'll find out who it is."

But Pressine knew Elinas would find nothing. Unwilling to contradict him, she stood and went to the window. She could see the raven still hanging outside her bedchamber window. Mattacks had manipulated his brother and meant this as a threat on her life.

Elinas rose and came behind her. "I am sorry for your loss, Pressine. I know you loved that raven."

"You have no idea how precious this bird was to me." Pressine repressed her grief. She could not reveal the magic nature of Ogyr. If it became public, the Christians would side with Mattacks to condemn her heathen ways. The kingdom needed unity, not division.

Turning to face Conan, Pressine could not be angry at him.

"I am truly sorry, my lady," the lad said softly. "I swear I did not know."

Pressine laid one hand on his shoulder. "I believe you Conan. Thank you for coming forward so quickly."

"I also believe you, son," the king rallied. "But for defying me and refusing to answer my questions, you deserve seven lashes, and you will stand for it under the oak by mid-morning."

Conan bowed. "As you wish, father." Turning around, he left the room without a word or a backward glance.

"Brave lad." Pressine had no doubt his brother put him up to it and could only guess how the boy must feel.

* * *

With a shiver of guilt, Pressine watched as Conan stood shirtless in the morning sun. A hooded soldier roped his wrists to a low branch of the oak, where he had committed his crime. The lad carried himself like an honorable man. Morgane stood at Pressine's side, and Ceinwyn held the wicker basket Pressine had prepared.

Among the assembled crowd looking on with reproach, Pressine saw servants and nobles, as well as guests who had come from remote estates to attend the wedding. The king's other children watched as well, even little Jared. The youngest prince still walked with crutches, but Pressine firmly believed he would fully recover.

Elinas was nowhere in sight. The king did not attend public punishments, unless they settled a matter of state.

Pressine's gaze fell on Mattacks, whose smile briefly turned into a smirk. The Edling must have known Conan would never rat on his own brother. The heir looked so cocksure, so proud of himself. Pressine wanted to see him take the punishment he deserved. But Mattacks manipulated people from the shadows, never exposed, never chastised.

Pressine caught Ceinwyn staring at the Edling with a smitten smile. How could she find him attractive? Of course, he had the charisma of a future king, and the girl could not possibly suspect his dark side. Mattacks looked very much like Elinas must have at his age.

A sigh from the crowd brought Pressine's attention back to Conan. The hooded soldier lifted the long leather whip. It cracked in the air once, catching the attention of any distracted onlooker. Pressine held her breath. The whip rose and fell, smarting flesh with a sickening sound.

Conan's muscles tensed but no cry escaped him. An angry red welt marred the fair skin of the prince's bare back.

As she could not see the boy's face, Pressine extended her senses to see him in her mind. She could feel his great pain and knew the lad bit his lips. Tears rolled down his cheeks, but he suffered in silence. Again, the whip lashed viciously. Pressine counted, five, six, seven.

The ordeal was over quickly and the crowd returned to more pressing occupations. When the hooded soldier untied Conan, Pressine rushed to support the young prince and, with the help of Morgane and Ceinwyn, laid him face down on the stone bench, in the shade. The lad did not protest.

From the basket she had prepared, Pressine took out a sponge and dipped it in a bowl of water and vinegar to wash away the blood. Conan jerked at the sting but did not cry out. Then Morgane applied a salve, and Ceinwyn bandaged the wounds. When Conan sat up, Pressine gave him a brew of willow bark to drink.

"I think I know what happened," Pressine told the boy as he sipped the bitter brew without recrimination. "I am sorry you had to go through this."

Conan smiled faintly. "It's over now," he said, pale as a sheet. "Will I have scars?"

"I hope not." The very thought horrified Pressine. "The salve should take care of that."

"Too bad." Conan grinned. "Scars are manly."

* * *

That afternoon, Mattacks observed at a distance a small party of women around a tiny balefire. He could not believe the witches were burning the bird on a pyre and praying for it. Then he remembered his mother, burned to ashes like a heathen. He had not been home to prevent it.

According to the church, women had no soul. Still, Mattacks wanted his mother to have a Christian burial, so she could be resurrected at the end of times. He also wished he had a grave stone to commemorate her existence. His father would pay dearly for this offense.

But first, Mattacks had a wedding to prevent, and only four days to do it.

Chapter Fourteen

On the morning of Ragnar's funeral, cold sunshine bathed the fortified Viking camp of Arstinchar. Gwenvael rejoiced at Bodvar's good spirits, as they walked side by side, the Viking prince with his left arm in a leather sling.

Gwenvael noticed Asa, Ragnar's chosen death wife, leaving a longhouse with a retinue and several guards.

"What is she doing?" Whatever it was, she didn't seem to enjoy it.

"She visits the thirteen warriors who meant the most to her lord, so they can honor him one last time through her." The wink of the single eye and the sensuous smile in Bodvar's blond beard told a lot about the nature of the honoring.

Gwenvael chuckled with embarrassment. "So, as his brother, you must be among the thirteen."

"Of course, I am." Bodvar laughed good heartedly. "And so are you."

"Me?" Shocked, Gwenvael did not comprehend. "I am not a warrior, and I did not know Ragnar that well."

"It is considered good luck to have a foreigner for the thirteenth lover," Bodvar explained, with enthusiasm. "To celebrate the strangeness of the thirteenth and last moon of the year. As the only free non-Viking in Arstinchar, you are the ideal thirteenth."

Gwenvael wanted to protest. But in matters of traditions, he had observed, it was wiser to conform.

Viking laws could condemn a man to death at the slightest infraction, so he remained quiet.

An hour later, Gwenvael and Bodvar waited in their longhouse, sipping mead on the platform bench of the central room. Gwenvael expected some protests from Cliona at this unusual duty of honoring the death bride. But the slave of many years, long familiar with Viking customs, expressed neither surprise nor objection. Not even jealousy.

When the death bride arrived with her entourage of women and warriors, the young girl bowed to Bodvar and followed him into his room. Meanwhile, the house slaves, Cliona included, served mead to the attendants waiting in the central room.

Gwenvael tried to ignore the grunts of pleasure or pain coming through the wall, wondering how Bodvar could manage. Hell, it was difficult enough to perform under such pressure, let alone with only one good arm. Gwenvael accepted yet another swig of the offered mead to muster his courage.

"Soon, you will drink like a true Viking!" The guard laughed and his friends joined in good-hearted approval.

After the sounds had died in the adjacent room, Asa came out alone, face flushed, her blonde hair in disarray. Straightening her white dress, she smiled timidly, her misty blue eyes small pools of despair.

Gwenvael could almost read her thoughts. Each lover brought her closer to death. She had already visited twelve, and Gwenvael was the last. By the holy relics, how could he possibly bed her now?

The frail lass gazed into his eyes. "I have come to do battle with you, my lord," she said in a controlled voice.

Gwenvael recognized the ritual phrase. Many Vikings, when talking about bedding a woman, used the same expression. Some said it was because the women fought, scratched, and bit like Berserkers under the spell of lovemaking.

But this death bride looked very tame indeed. With the most comforting smile he could manage, Gwenvael led Asa to his room, opposite Bodvar's. A glance at Cliona as he closed the leather curtain told him nothing of her feelings.

Without a word, the lass promptly removed her dress and lay on the fur pallet, exposing her tiny breasts, protruding ribs, and slim hairless body. She looked very different from Cliona, yet beautiful in her youth and vulnerability.

"Do not hurry on my account." Gwenvael sat next to her and lifted a strand of blond hair from her face. "I want to give you as much time as you like."

Tears swelled at the rim of her wide blue eyes as she sat up. "Thank you." She buried her face in his chest. "I am so scared."

Gwenvael drew her into his arms. How he wanted to protect her from such a grim fate. But he knew no one could. He thought about converting her to Christianity, but there was no time to explain such abstract concepts. It would only spread doubt in her mind and rob her of her only immediate comfort, the certainty of the reward from the gods she believed in.

"We do not have to do battle if you do not want to." Gwenvael caressed her hair.

"But I want to." She gripped his tunic. "Anything to occupy my mind and forget what comes next." She pressed her open mouth to his lips in a wanton kiss.

Aroused by the girl's desperation, Gwenvael answered in kind, but he controlled his ardor to concentrate on giving her pleasure. Remembering the many techniques he had learned from Cliona, he caressed her small breasts, the sensitive skin under her arms, the inside of her thighs, creating a greater need that would heighten her release.

Asa moaned, arching under his hands, and ripped open the front of his tunic to scratch the muscles of his chest. Gwenvael had to exert supreme control not to take her then. Enjoying her exalted state, he brought it to a paroxysm and had her screaming for release, but still he would not take her.

Holding her tight under him, hands probing, lips kissing, and teeth biting in strategic places, he overwhelmed her and felt her respond, her sensations heightened by the knowledge of her imminent death. Without taking off his clothes, he kept pleasuring her relentlessly.

Finally, Asa's surprisingly strong hands jerked the string of his trews and pulled them down. Gwenvael's painful erection could not be denied any longer. In a desperate thrust, he entered her silky vault, provoking another flurry of screams.

Nails scratched his back and buttocks, teeth bit his hard nipples, but he did not relent. Holding his release, he kept plowing vigorously. Three times he felt the flood of her pleasure heat, before gratifying himself. But still it was not enough.

Upon Asa's urging, Gwenvael resumed his thrust. This time he found it easier to hold back while performing with the level of intensity to match the girl's need. Catching his second wind, Gwenvael brought her to four more releases before allowing his own.

Falling back upon the fleece, Asa sighed and smiled contentedly. "I shall tell my prince that you honored him well." She kissed his hand.

Gwenvael noticed the blue lines of exhaustion under her eyes as she closed them briefly. What a shame to kill such a lass. He wished for the power to change things, but he knew he could not. He caressed her cheek and kissed her brow. Casually, he let his right thumb trace the sign of the cross on her forehead.

God all forgiving, please accept this innocent lamb into the heavens. Gwenvael hoped the Almighty would accept these unconventional last rites. Then he set about retrieving clothes he did not remember shedding.

"I am ready for the potion now," Asa said seriously. "This is all I want to remember."

"The potion?" Gwenvael shivered. "You are not going to kill yourself, are you?" That would be a deadly sin.

"No... I do not have that kind of courage." Asa smiled sadly. "The potion from the Angel of Death will only numb my mind and make it easier to die."

But even that fact did not lighten Gwenvael's heavy heart.

* * *

The Nagelfar buzzed with flies, and the breeze moved the flaps of the funeral tent erected on the aft deck. As an official witness, Gwenvael watched the approaching cortege, trying to ignore the stench of slaughter house. On the lower deck, quartered horses and sacrificed sheep, goats, and pigs lay in a gruesome pile.

Supported by two sturdy warriors, Asa staggered as she crossed the assembled crowd and ascended the gangplank. Her half closed eyes and lolling head told Gwenvael the potion had done its work. Framed by Bodvar and Sigurd, the commander of the new fleet, Gwenvael stared helplessly as the warriors set the lass on the couch, next to the decomposing prince.

A white veil enveloped Ragnar's face, alive from the constant crawling of maggots. Asa did not seem to mind. The Angel of Death arranged the white flimsy dress along the richly attired cadaver in yellow silk and fine leather boots. A sword had been fastened to the prince's hand.

When the crone pulled a dagger from the folds of her dress, Gwenvael held his breath. He remembered Asa, clawing at him and screaming her passion, just a few minutes ago. Why extinguish such a delightful woman?

Tears flowed down his cheeks and he let them drop to the rich Persian rug. Someday, he would put an end to these barbaric customs and replace them with Christian love. But it would take time.

With a horrible scream, the Angel of Death drove the dagger between Asa's ribs while a warrior strangled the lass from behind with a thin seal rope.

Despite his grief, Gwenvael forced himself to watch. The death bride tensed slightly then relaxed and lay peaceful as an angel of God. *Forgive me, Asa, for not being able to save you.* Holding back sobs, Gwenvael prayed for the repose of her soul.

While officiates and witnesses left the ship, Gwenvael and Bodvar helped the chosen warriors unfurl the sail. It flapped and caught the wind. They secured sail and rudder, splashed a barrel of lamp oil on the deck, then disembarked. After throwing aside the plank, they removed the blocks of wood that stabilized the Nagelfar on dry sand. Then the thirteen warriors, Gwenvael included, pushed the Drakkar out to sea.

As the boat floated in shallow water, Bodvar handed Gwenvael a flaming torch. "You should throw it in... For good luck."

Nodding, Gwenvael accepted the torch. He wanted this morbid spectacle to be over. Closing his eyes, he threw the flaming brand over the rail.

Black smoke rose, and the sound of cracking wood filled the air. Quickly the fire spread to the tent on the aft deck. As the stench of burning flesh pervaded the beach, Gwenvael struggled to overcome his revulsion.

A breeze caught the sail and the Nagelfar picked up speed. Soon, billows of smoke rose to the clear sky. Fed by the wind, the flames grew taller and licked the frame of the funeral tent. And the longship sailed away, like a fiery dragon, smoking and belching angry fire.

Overflowing with grief, Gwenvael prayed for the dead and for the living. *Dear God, have mercy on their souls.*

* * *

That night, the level of rejoicing reached its climax in the Viking chieftain's hall. Bodvar presided, drinking heavily of nabid, the special beer reserved for funerals. No herring or haddock that night, but chewy horsemeat, sweet reindeer, and even bear. Gwenvael enjoyed the food, slowly getting used to the Viking way of boiling or steaming the meat rather than roasting it.

Well into the feasting, cheeks ruddy from strong beer, eye patch slightly askew, Bodvar rose clumsily, compensating for his restrained left arm. He demanded silence by banging the handle of his battle axe on the wooden floor. Having obtained a relative degree of quiet, he spoke in a booming voice.

"Tonight, we celebrate more than my brother's journey to Valhalla." Bodvar's single eye surveyed the generals and their female slaves. "The friend who saved my life twice and found Ragnar's body has asked me a favor that goes against our customs."

A murmur of protest greeted the announcement.

"Cliona, you Briton wench," Bodvar called gruffly.

A warm glow on her face, Cliona glanced at Gwenvael questioningly then rose to obey her prince.

"I shall miss you, but the time has come to part." Bodvar shoved her down. "Kneel, slave!"

Cliona obeyed the strange order.

"Someone bring me a chopping block."

A warrior promptly brought a sturdy piece of wood, streaked with blood from the ceremonial offerings. He set it in front of Cliona.

The small hair on Gwenvael's nape suddenly rose in alarm. Would Bodvar rather kill Cliona than free her?

Bodvar motioned to Sigurd who nodded and took Bodvar's battle axe. "I would do this myself, but I might miss." Bodvar motioned to his bound arm.

The comment brought a raucous laugh from the warriors.

Sigurd positioned Cliona's red head for execution.

Gwenvael's blood went cold. He felt paralyzed. *Please, God, not her!*

Moving her slave necklet to one side, Sigurd pushed her long hair away from her milky neck, then hefted the weapon, measuring the blow.

Gwenvael would have fainted, if not for the beer horn someone handed him. He took it with a trembling hand. In the silent hall, time stood still as Sigurd raised the axe. The blow fell with a dry thud and a clink of metal.

Gwenvael screamed, his scream drowned in the cheer of the warriors around him.

Cliona rose slowly, leaving on the wooden platform her bondage necklet severed by the axe. Tears filled her eyes as she gazed at Gwenvael, then she bowed to all the men and women in the hall.

Cliona dropped a light kiss on Bodvar's blond beard, to the hoots of the other Vikings. "Thank you my prince."

Gwenvael exulted, the blood in his veins running cold and hot. He raised his drinking horn then drained it.

When Bodvar called his name, Gwenvael rose on unsteady feet and joined Cliona's side.

Taking both their hands in his huge paw, Bodvar declared, "Since it is your wish, and the wish of such a loyal friend cannot be ignored, I hereby marry you, Gwenvael and Cliona, both members of my household."

Upon a sign from Bodvar, two Vikings volunteered their drinking horns for the couple. Someone took Gwenvael's empty one and replaced it with a full horn. Following Bodvar's directions, each lover drank first from separate cups, then switched and drank again. Finally, linking their arms, they finished both cups under the benevolent gaze of the chieftains, who hailed when they finished.

Heart pummeling his chest, Gwenvael dug into the fold of his tunic, fishing for the gold bracelet he had kept for just the right moment. "Your wedding bracelet," he announced, sliding the coiled golden serpent on Cliona's bare arm, high above the elbow.

Bodvar motioned to a slave who brought a bundle and presented it to Cliona. She opened it, revealing a new dress. Not the slaves' coarse brown wool, but a fine garment of bright emerald green to match her eyes.

"Now," Bodvar declared to the assembly, "as a free and married woman, you owe Cliona the respect you give to your own wives. May I remind you that the law dictates to hang by the neck he who forces a free woman in a Viking camp."

A murmur of agreement ran among the revelers.

"But if she requests your loving services, of course, you should do your best to keep her satisfied.

Soldiers' wives can get lonely, and all we want is their happiness." Bodvar drained his drinking horn.

"I have a wife at home, too." Bodvar's voice took on a nostalgic tone, probably due to the mead. "I hope the many bastards she conceived in my absence grow fat on the plunder I send her."

The warriors cheered.

Bodvar stopped a serving slave. "Now, bring more food and more mead. By Thor, this is a funeral! Everyone should celebrate!"

Such strange customs. Gwenvael had a lot of work ahead to bring Christianity to the Vikings. He only hoped the sins of these barbarians would not compromise or tarnish his immortal soul.

As the Vikings returned to their jolly feasting, Gwenvael locked Cliona in a tight embrace, listening to both hearts beating like two hammers on the same anvil. Here, at the northernmost tip of Scott territory, in the Viking enclave of Arstinchar, he had found the happiness he never dared hope for. He'd found the opportunity to serve the Christian god, the freedom to love and live, and start a family with this wonderful wife.

Chapter Fifteen

By the flickering candlelight of his chambers, Mattacks assessed the young Christian baron who squirmed in the high back chair. How eager was he to please his future king?

"If you perform this task without mishap..." Standing with his back to the hearth, Mattacks paused for emphasis. "I shall secure your future among my favorite councilors."

Urien of Lanark, brushed a crumb off his fine maroon wool trews and cleared his throat. "This is quite a daring enterprise, my prince."

Soft rain pattered against the closed shutters, the only sound in the castle at this late hour. Mattacks added a log to the crackling fire.

"Take time to weigh the risks against the rewards, Urien." Mattacks wiped his hands on a silk handkerchief. "Once on the throne, I can grant you anything."

"But, a future queen..." The young baron's hazel gaze wandered from the wall tapestries to the floor rug, as if searching for clues.

Checking the shutters, Mattacks closed the heavy drapes against possible spies. "She is only an obscure foreign princess, disowned by her father."

"Still." The young baron's Adam's apple bobbed as he swallowed hard.

Smiling encouragingly, Mattacks sat on the massive oak table and faced Urien. "Will you want more lands, with the privilege to collect taxes?"

Urien's expression remained closed.

"Perhaps you need funds for a monastery, with genuine relics... or a magnificent church with a bishopric for your beautiful town of Lanark?"

A sudden gleam of interest lit Urien's eyes.

"Or you might prefer an army to carve yourself a small kingdom? Or one of my sisters in marriage?" Mattacks enjoyed the battle raging on the young baron's face. Greed against fear.

The two youths understood each other well. Same age, same religious fervor, same pride and ambition. But Mattacks knew how to use men, while Urien followed like a hound, happy to snatch table scraps from his master's hand.

Urien's eyes narrowed. "What if I get caught?" He flinched at a loud pop when cinder sparked from the smoky fire. "Queen or not, the king will have me executed for treason."

"My father upholds the traditional law, which does not protect foreigners, as I shall remind him if it comes to pass." Had Mattacks made a mistake in choosing Urien of Lanark? "Besides, you cannot get caught if you use a discreet intermediary to hire a handful of brigands for the job."

Mattacks filled pewter goblets with wine from the ewer and pushed one toward Urien. "That way, no one can connect you to the deed, even if the churls are caught."

Urien considered his goblet but did not touch it. "Perhaps, it could work."

"Think." Mattacks drank one long sip before admonishing his coup de grâce. "God will protect you while you do His work. There is no higher purpose.

Bishop Renald highly recommended you for the task and has already granted absolution."

"The order comes from the bishop?" Urien of Lanark stared, mouth half open, visibly shaken.

"Yes. But he cannot be compromised. He should in no way be associated with this mission." Mattacks rose and paced the room to cover his blatant lie. He hoped God would absolve the small sin for the success of His greater purpose. "If asked, even by you, Renald will adamantly deny any knowledge of it. In his heart, however, he relies upon us to rid the kingdom of the devil-spawn."

Urien looked baffled, raking his hair with nervous fingers. "I had no idea I would be working for Rome."

Positioning himself behind the young baron's chair, Mattacks used a tone of confidentiality. "Given the present circumstances, my father may not be in power very long. Think of what happens when I become king and you already handle my most sensitive affairs."

"The offer sounds very attractive, my prince." Urien pulled down his embroidered sleeve. "I happen to know a capable and discreet man, who would welcome a handsome payment to make a mere woman disappear."

Mattacks grinned at his victory. "I knew I could count on your loyalty!"

Urien of Lanark straightened in his chair. "What does the bishop want done with the heathen bitch?"

Savoring the thought, Mattacks spoke casually. "Have your man cut her tongue, dress her in rags, and sell her to slave traders in Northumbria."

Urien seemed shocked but recovered quickly. "A slave?"

"She is young and pretty enough to fetch a good price."

Urien drummed well-groomed fingernails on the table. "It may take time to assemble such men."

"You only have two days." Mattacks stared into the young baron's eyes. "You must carry out the task before she becomes queen."

"I understand." Urien hesitated then took a deep breath and released it slowly. "It will be done as the bishop ordered."

"Good." Mattacks struggled to keep his excitement under control. "In any case," he said with a calm he did not feel, "make sure the hired help never suspects who the lady is. Suffice it to tell them where she sleeps. There are no guards at her door or windows, and only very young servants sleeping in the adjacent rooms."

Urien dripped with new importance. "My men can enter the fort with the extra kitchen help during the day. At night, they strike and carry away their prize over the wall. What about the guards on the ramparts?"

Mattacks could not suppress a grin. "I shall make sure they receive an ample supply of celebration wine." He winked. "Laced with a sleeping draught."

Mattacks weighed the heavy purse at his belt. "Someone outside should be waiting with ladders. And fast horses. Riding all night, the captors will be far away by morning. The bride will not be found. Hence, no wedding and no heathen queen."

Urien of Lanark eyed the purse intently. "Surely, the king will send search parties."

"You and I will volunteer and lead them astray." Mattacks dropped the purse on the massive table and pushed it toward Urien. "This should buy everything you need."

Urien smiled his approval. "Very cunning." He patted the purse. "And very generous, my prince."

Mattacks raised his cup. "Under our vigilance, Christendom will prevail."

"Amen!" hailed the young baron, then he drained his goblet.

Grinning, Mattacks congratulated himself on this clever scheme.

* * *

Pressine's heart beat so fast, she could not sleep. Tomorrow, she would marry her king. Did she hear something outside? Whispers? Hurried footsteps?

She flung the blankets aside, walked to the window and opened the shutters but all was quiet. The memory of her dead raven hanging outside the window made her uneasy. The snarling face of Mattacks appeared in her mind. The Edling would try to prevent the wedding.

A balmy summer breeze had blown away the rain clouds of the previous days and the moonlight could not eclipse the many stars. Far into the night, a dog howled at the moon. Toward the kitchen midden, toads sang in deep throaty notes, competing with the trills of the nightingale. At the mournful hoot of an owl, all sounds stopped. Why?

All senses alert, Pressine held her breath, listening for clues, watching. There it was, a quiet shuffle. Suddenly, Pressine felt alone and vulnerable. Before she could close the shutters, a shadow jumped through the window, then another.

A hand muffled Pressine's scream. Another hand grabbed her waist. She saw the glint of a knife in the moonlight. She slapped and hit and kicked, but the men holding her were too strong.

A stone throw away across the courtyard, the king's window faced her own, but its shutters remained tightly closed. If only she could... *Please, Elinas, wake up!*

As she struggled against the table, her hand knocked the fruit bowl. Her fingers closed on a small crab apple, smooth and hard to the touch. She did not have time to aim or evaluate the distance, but she had been good at this in her childhood games. She threw with all her strength. The hard fruit banged against the king's shutters and bounced off.

"Bitch!" The man holding her twisted her arm back.

Pressine cried in pain, but the sound barely escaped the hand sealing her lips. A man seized her feet. Another shadow provided a large sac. No! As she fought back, Pressine stared at the king's window. *Elinas, please...*

A candle flickered behind the slats. The shutters slammed open and Elinas appeared in a night shirt. "Who dares disturb the king's sleep?"

"The king?" Muffled cries, an oath cut short. The men let go of Pressine and climbed out the window.

Elinas raised his candle. "Who's there?" His commanding voice cut like a blade through the still night.

"Over there," Pressine shouted. "Do not let them escape. They attacked me."

The king turned inside and called, "Guards!"

Pressine exhaled a sigh of relief. Would the guards catch her attackers? Would the churls incriminate Mattacks and open the king's eyes on the evil nature of his son?

The outside doors to the king's chambers burst open, and royal guards spilled into the courtyard. One of them lit the torches hanging along the walls, while others beat the thicket, thrusting spear or sword through every shrub, into every dark recess, behind every tree.

Coming out of his chambers into the courtyard, Elinas buckled his sword belt on hastily drawn trews. "What in Bel's name is going on?"

The captain of the guards ran up to the king. "Marauders, My Lord."

"Where are the sentries? Why did no one sound the alarm? A silver coin for every marauder caught!"

A horn resounded, awakening the whole fortress. More horns responded.

Pressine rushed out of her chambers to meet Elinas in the courtyard.

"Pressine, my love, are you safe?" The king sounded relieved to see her unharmed.

"Yes my lord." She attempted a smile.

"The gods be thanked." Elinas enveloped her in his arms.

"But not for your quick response, they might have succeeded in carrying me away." Pressine did not mention her gifts. In any case, she could not use them for selfish ends, only in the service of the Goddess.

"Whoever dared do this will pay dearly for it." Elinas tightened his grasp on her. "I could not stand it if anything happened to you."

"Obviously, someone does not want me to be queen." Pressine refrained to accuse Mattacks. She had no proof. How brazen of him to mount such a direct assault on her person inside the castle.

Elinas walked Pressine back to her chambers. "You will be safe with my personal guards at each door and window. But right now, I must find out why the ramparts are not guarded."

Pressine gripped his arm. "Be careful, my lord."

Elinas smiled. "As always."

"And let me know what you find out." She smiled back to soften the request.

"I will." Kissing her forehead, Elinas walked out into the courtyard.

Pressine shivered with dread at the thought of what could have happened. She might be safe for the rest of the night, but what kind of dangers was she walking into by marrying Elinas?

* * *

Mattacks repressed an oath at the sudden activity in the courtyard. No one was supposed to find out until morning. Praying Urien had not botched the job, he buckled his sword belt with trembling fingers. How could the incompetent sot jeopardize Mattacks' greatest dreams?

He hoped he could correct the blunder by covering the kidnappers' tracks. Next time, he would remember not to trust an inexperienced whelp. Pulling on his riding gloves, Mattacks stepped out of his chambers.

He stopped the captain who dispatched the guards.

"What is the disturbance?" Mattacks hoped the captain would interpret his uneasiness as legitimate concern.

"Intruders, my prince." The sturdy captain in red tunic and mail, grim under the helmet, looked stunned by the audacity of the deed. "Near the King's chambers, no less. Just escaped over the wall."

Mattacks wanted to know if Pressine was missing but could not ask. "Anybody hurt?"

"No, my prince." The captain said with obvious relief. "They were interrupted and ran away. The king ordered a search beyond the walls."

Mattacks dared to hope. If Pressine's absence had not been discovered, his plan might still hold.

"Do not bother, Captain, I will search the countryside," he declared with a magnanimous smile. "Keep your guards inside to stand watch on the king, and tell Urien of Lanark to meet me at the stables with his men."

"Thank you, my prince." The captain bowed with a small smile of gratitude. "The king will appreciate your help. You should have seen how upset he was when Lady Pressine told him what happened."

So, Urien had failed! Damn the whole bunch of them for ruining Mattacks' last chance to prevent the wedding.

"I see..." But Mattacks could not understand how a lowly woman could have thwarted the carefully planned abduction. Unless the devil himself was helping her! That must be it.

The captain saluted. "I must go."

"Thank you, Captain." Mattacks masked his anger under a forced smile and a friendly wave of the hand.

How he hated himself for having underestimated the evil bitch. By becoming queen tomorrow, she would grow into a formidable opponent, and he could do nothing to prevent it.

Mattacks kicked a clump of dirt as he marched toward the stables. It might take all his cleverness to get rid of the heathen shrew, but he swore before God Almighty that he would find a way, even if it took months or years to succeed.

* * *

In a gold wedding dress mirroring the radiance of the midday sun, black hair flowing below a crown of primrose, daisies, snapdragons, heather and forget-me-nots, Pressine slowly walked beside Elinas. Ahead of the royal bride and groom, three young pages, dressed in blue, threw handfuls of white petals in their path.

As they crossed the castle grounds, Pressine could feel all the eyes fixed on her, judging her, loving her... or hating her. The king, in red and black silk, a gold circlet on his dark brow, nodded right and left, smiling at tribal kings and barons and waving to old friends. Pressine smiled to familiar faces on the way to the great white canopy stretched over the partially erected walls of the future chapel.

Despite the perspiration dripping under the polished helmets, the royal guard stood motionless on each side of the path in two perfect rows. Spear points bright, armored shields straight and evenly spaced, they contained the crowd of invited guests.

On both sides of the path formed by the guards, ladies in vermillion and yellow silk smiled and curtsied as the couple walked by. Men in deep green and purple bowed respectfully. The cheerful chords of stringed instruments from the troupe of minstrels accompanied the slow march.

From the kitchens wafted the aroma of roasting meat and baking pies.

Power always came at a price, and Pressine knew that better than anyone. The fright of the previous night seemed a faraway memory, like a nightmare that fades and vanishes in daylight. This marriage would make her Queen of Strathclyde. But soon, as planned by the Goddess, when Elinas rallied Britons, Scots, Picts, and Angles, today's bride would also become the High Queen of Alba.

The couple stopped in front of a dais where the old druid in white flowing robes waited beside a tree stump. Long white hair tousled by the gentle breeze, he smiled kindly from his high platform. His dark eyes twinkled as they rested on Pressine. The bride and groom ascended the nine steps of the dais to face the druid.

After sprinkling spring water to the four horizons, the old man took Pressine's left hand and Elinas' right. With a braided rope of mixed green grasses, he tied their wrists together with a knot. Pressine relished the contact of her king's hand as he squeezed hers. Then the druid circled the couple three times sunwise, arms open wide, chanting ancient incantations.

A manservant joined them on the dais, carrying a bleating white goat, then laid the struggling animal on the tree stump and held it. The wood block looked almost black, stained by the blood of past sacrifices. Clasping the silver sickle hooked at his belt, the Druid slashed the goat's throat in one sure stroke. Blood spurted then pooled in the nooks and crannies of the stump. The animal's limbs twitched in the throes of death.

Blood smeared his white robes. Then the druid faced the couple again and spoke in a fierce voice belying his age. "In the name of Bel of the dreadful eye, and Lugh the shiny one, and Oghma who invented the alphabet, I hereby witness this couple's nuptial vows. Do you promise to love and support each other until death?"

"I promise," said Elinas in a firm voice.

"I promise," Pressine said in turn.

"May this union so please our gods that they spread their bounty on the land."

Turning toward the goat, the Druid sliced open its belly, spilling the steamy innards in an untidy pile of slippery entrails. As he knelt to study the viscous mess, Pressine could see from his blank expression that the old man had entered a trance. Then, his jaw tightened and a shadow crossed his face. Pressine shuddered and wondered what he had seen but dare not ask.

Rising, the druid faced the couple gravely. Staring at both of them in turn, he said in a barely audible voice, "May all promises be kept in this world, as in the otherworld." He untied their wrists, gave the grass rope to Pressine, then bowed as he presented the newlyweds to the cheering crowd.

Under a shower of white flowers, the royal pair descended from the dais. Banners fluttered from neighboring trees and poles. Minstrels played the flute as Pressine walked with Elinas toward the open canopy covering the site of the future chapel.

Sections of free standing walls, partial columns and low buttresses were decorated with lengths of white cloth and flower garlands. Piles of cut sandstones lay at regular intervals to mark the perimeter of the future building. From a temporary pedestal at the entrance of the future nave, the statue of the Great Goddess guarded the sprouting edifice.

The fact that the bishop persisted in calling Her the Black Madonna had not deterred Morgane, who somehow had obtained Renald's permission to give her blessing in front of the statue. No doubt the bishop allowed it, hoping some miracle would lead to Morgane's conversion. Little did he know.

Although smaller than the looming statue behind her, Morgane seemed to glow. Lithe and dark in her silky blue shift, she looked like the Great Goddess, black hair parted in the middle and gathered in a single braid down her back. Could anyone else see the striking resemblance? Since Pressine looked so much like her aunt Morgane, she realized with a start that she, too, must resemble the Goddess.

Eyes the color of mist, the Great Priestess of the Lost Isle gazed at the approaching couple. When she raised one hand, gesturing the bride and groom to go no further, silence fell on the assembled guests. Pressine could not remember when the minstrels had stopped playing. No one spoke or moved, as if time stood still.

"King of Strathclyde," Morgane heralded with authority. "Are you willing to serve the Great Goddess who yearns to lavish Her boons on this land and protect it from foreign invaders, drought, blight, and pestilence?"

"I am willing."

"Do you wed this woman to share with her your victorious crown?"

"I do wed her."

"Do you swear never to lay eyes on her in childbed?"

Elinas turned to Pressine, a puzzled look on his face. Surely he could not have forgotten the curse. She smiled encouragements.

Elinas turned back to Morgane. "I swear it."

"Do you promise to treat her as an equal?"

Elinas raised a questioning brow then shrugged. "I promise."

Now facing Pressine, Morgane announced, "Pressine of Bretagne, Lady of the Lost Isle, do you swear to love, help, and protect your king and husband in his sacred quest, by all means available to your kind, in the love of the Great Goddess, as long as your husband lives?"

"I swear it."

Morgane nodded. "In the name of the Great Goddess, I declare you bound in wedlock, king and

241

queen in this world and the next. But if you ever break any of these oaths, be prepared to suffer the wrath of the Goddess. She will wrench you apart, blight your land, curse the royal lineage through the ninth generation, and you will know only grief and torment until one of you dies, freeing the other from this sacred bond."

As Morgane receded behind the statue of the Goddess, leaving the wedding guests in bewildered silence, Pressine's heart faltered. Not until now had she understood the gravity of the curse. The fate of the entire kingdom was at stake.

Grasping her king's arm for reassurance, Pressine glanced up and caught his stunned expression. Elinas covered her hand with his, then guided her down the future nave toward the Christian altar. To the monotone chant of visiting monks in brown robes standing behind the altar, the crowd followed the royal pair under the canopy.

There, on white linen, shadowed by a tall crucifix, a plate and a chalice of polished gold reflected the flickering flames of two white tallow candles. To the side, lay a large open book. Standing in front of the altar, Bishop Renald looked pale, white knuckles gripping his crozier. He greeted the couple with a nod then straightened the miter on his head.

Renald had accepted to perform the sacred ritual although they were not baptized, in hopes to rally new voices to the Christian cause. Pressine had accepted. Politics applied to every aspect of a queen's life, even religion. She also understood the importance of rituals.

At least, there would be no holy water. Pressine had insisted upon that point. In occasions, holy water was rumored to have burned Faery born women like quick lime. Because of his gender, Gwenvael had survived baptism with holy water, but he had lost all his supernatural powers. Pressine would rather not chance either on her wedding day.

The sacristan came and waved a censer at the end of a chain in front of the bride and groom. Clouds of Myrrh-scented smoke floated toward the white canopy. Next, the man walked the crowd's perimeter to incense the assembly.

"Kneel to show humility before the Almighty," Renald uttered in a bland voice.

Pressine knelt. So did Elinas. The bishop walked to the end of the altar, where the great book lay open. His back to the crowd, the bishop chanted verses in bad church Latin that grated on Pressine's ears. From time to time, he turned to address the Christian crowd, which answered his prompts by mumbling the appropriate lines.

Although not interested in the Christian ceremony, Pressine wished her brother Gwenvael could see it. He would certainly approve. She observed Elinas. He did not pay attention to the bishop either, as if his mind wandered far away. A light brush of the hand brought him back to the present.

The litanies went on so long that Pressine's knees started to hurt, even on the rush protecting them from the hard ground. Sometimes the bishop genuflected and kissed the book, sometimes he mumbled to himself. At other times, he shouted the ritual words at the top of his lungs. Finally, he approached the couple.

"Please rise," he said, simply.

As Pressine stood up on stiff legs, Elinas supported her arm.

"Elinas of Dumfries, King of Strathclyde, will you take this woman for wife and queen, honoring and protecting her until death, according to the rules of Our Holy Mother Church?"

"I will." Elinas sounded so solemn.

"Pressine of Bretagne, will you take this man for husband and king, serve him and honor him in obedience and humility until death, according to the rules of Our Holy Mother Church?"

"I will." Obedience and humility clashed with the previous vows of equality, but Pressine just wanted to be done with the ritual.

Dipping his right thumb in a bowl of scented oil carried by the sacristan, Bishop Renald anointed the king's forehead then Pressine's with the sign of the cross. Taking the chalice from the altar, the bishop drank from it some of the blood-red wine, then passed it to the king who took a sip, and finally to Pressine who did the same. Thank the Goddess, the blessed wine did not burn her throat.

Taking the golden plate, Renald broke a piece of bread and ate it, then gave a piece to the king, and a piece to Pressine.

As she ate and drank what should be the blood and body of Christ, Pressine tried to imagine the Christian god, the Holy Host, coming into her. But she found no magic in the food or drink. To her surprise, no enhanced awareness came with the communion bread. So much for the depth of Christian mysteries.

In her mother's realm, the Ladies similarly ate the food of the gods, the Manna, baked with the white gold powder, to maintain their mystical powers and longevity. Pressine rarely partook of the divine food, but saturated with it in the womb, she remained strong and her powers needed very little to go on.

Finally, placing a gold circlet on Pressine's brow, the bishop declared in a loud voice, "I pronounce you King and Queen in the eyes of God, in the name of the Father, the Son, and the Holy Spirit!"

A loud "Amen!" from the crowd concluded the ritual.

Pressine and Elinas turned to face their subjects. Among the applause, a gleeful Hallelujah resounded from the choir of monks. Several Christian guests joined in the hymn.

Hanging onto her king's arm, Pressine walked out of the white canopy, nodding to the statue of the Goddess. Elinas led her along the path delineated by the royal guard, toward a dais erected under the great oak. Pressine smiled and waved at the festive guests.

Banners streamed from the venerable branches as Pressine sat with Elinas on the crimson pillows of two heavily cushioned chairs, to receive homage. Soon, barons, tribal kings and princes lined up to renew their allegiance.

With an irrepressible grin, Elinas introduced to Pressine a few royal guests she had not met. She was delighted to see old Dewain again as he offered his warmest congratulations. The king's children joined the crowd to pay respects. Little Jared still limped a little from the accident in the mill, and young Conan had tears in his eyes when he kissed Pressine's hand.

On this peaceful day of celebration and religious tolerance, only one shadow darkened the horizon.

Mattacks knelt before his father and kissed Caliburn's point to pledge allegiance. When the Edling stood, Elinas turned and conversed with Dewain, who had joined his side.

Mattacks faced Pressine squarely, unblinking, without as much as a bow, a look of pure hatred on his face. Although deeply shaken by the blatant insult, Pressine nodded and smiled bravely, as to a beloved stepson. Unfortunately, Elinas saw nothing of Mattacks' insulting attitude.

What could Pressine do to impress on Elinas the dangerous nature of his son?

* * *

Later, in the hall, at the high table, the troubadours played the flute and string instruments to accompany the good food and wine. While Morgane talked with the old druid and with Dewain, Mattacks engaged in conversation with Bishop Renald.

Turning to Elinas, Pressine whispered, "Any trace of last night's intruders?"

The king shook his head. "The guards had too much wine and fell asleep. They will be chastised for it."

"What about the pursuit?"

"Mattacks and Lord Urien of Lanark searched all night with their men but found no trace of the fugitives" Elinas shook his head. "The tracks stopped at the river and the hounds lost the scent."

Pressine bristled inwardly. Elinas did not suspect his son. But if Mattacks had hired the miscreants, of course he would misdirect the search.

Did Urien of Lanark support the Edling against her? As a staunch Christian, he might.

"Perhaps you need more experienced men to lead the search, lord husband," she suggested with a smile, "like the Baron of Ayre."

"I like the title of husband." Elinas squeezed Pressine's hand and smiled. "But Dewain does not relish such arduous work anymore. It is time for young men to take over the chores."

"Of course. You know best. Who do you think is responsible?"

Elinas shrugged. "I have many enemies, but these particular miscreants are long gone. Believe me, they will not return anytime soon."

"But what if they do? Or what if they have accomplices inside the walls?" Pressine glanced in the direction of Mattacks. The Edling paid no attention to the royal couple.

"I doubled the guard. It will not happen again." Elinas kissed her fingers. "I assure you that we are now quite safe."

Pressine hid her disappointment. She knew that voicing her suspicions without proof would only upset Elinas and make her seem hostile for no reason. She would bide her time and wait for Mattacks to make a mistake.

But this was her wedding day, and she would not let anything spoil it. Her mind reeled with so many exciting thoughts. She flushed at the prospect of her wedding night.

Pressine tingled with anticipation, dizzy from the strong wine. Despite the spinach and egg flat cakes, the fattened goose and the roasted piglet, she felt the effects of the potent drink. Before taking another sip from the royal cup, Pressine turned it deliberately and looked into the soft brown eyes of her king, drinking where his lips had touched.

A slight blush colored Elinas' tanned cheeks. He smiled devilishly. "Now, this is no behavior befitting a chaste lady."

"Perish the thought I would remain chaste for long!" Pressine winked. "I intend to find out for myself what everyone is talking and smiling about."

It dawned on Pressine that she knew little of human amorous behavior beyond a brush of the fingers, a secret embrace, or a kiss. She had witnessed an equine mating once, long ago, in a dewy pasture of her native Bretagne. Heat suffused her cheeks at the flaring of wild feelings the memory brought.

While the guests enjoyed the banquet with boisterous stories, toasts, and good wishes for the couple, Pressine suddenly wished she knew more about the details of a wedding night. Busy with all the preparations, she had forgotten to ask Morgane.

Chapter Sixteen

Elinas deposited Pressine at the foot of her bed then walked back to the massive door and lifted the heavy locking bar into its supports. It fell into place with a metallic clang. The events of the night before had left him shaken. He had no inkling of who would want to harm his bride, although he could guess why.

Pressine had grown quiet and watched him, her eyes shiny in the soft candlelight.

"I want no interruption tonight." He flashed an apologetic smile.

He hoped she could not see the tension clutching the muscles of his jaw as he closed the shutters and drapes. He lifted every wall hanging, hand on Caliburn's hilt, taut as a high-strung cat, ready to slit any intruder's throat.

"I hate nasty surprises. Too many strangers on the grounds tonight. I cannot take any chances," he said in what he hoped was a reassuring tone.

As he stoked the crackling fire, Elinas hid his struggle for self control. Despite his aching need, he did not trust his ability to satisfy this bride. It had been so long since he last made love, and over eighteen years since deflowering his late queen, the only virgin he had ever touched. At the time, in the impatience of youth, he had probably rushed the task.

Although he felt nervous as a lad facing his first woman, he must exude strength, confidence, reassurance. The last thing he wanted to do was alienate his young bride by a clumsy joining.

"Do you like incense?" He struggled to control his shaky hands as he reached for the richly decorated leather pouch on the table. "I obtained a rare batch of Myrrh from a trader in Whithorn."

"What a wonderful gift, my lord. It must have cost a fortune." Pressine sat gracefully on the bed and arranged her dress around her. When she looked up at him, her clear gray eyes sparkled. "My father used to burn Myrrh on special occasions. I have not enjoyed it in a long time."

Opening the pouch, Elinas took a few of the golden crystals and threw them on the embers. Hissing on contact, they released a light smoke that filled the room with sweet fragrance.

"The scent is delightful," Pressine closed her eyes briefly.

Elinas inhaled the pleasing essence to calm his restless nerves, then exhaled slowly. He unbuckled his baldric, hung it to the sculpted high back of a chair, then removed his coat and tossed the crimson and black garment upon the same chair.

Walking toward the bed where Pressine sat, he found it easy to smile. He would win her, body and soul. The unconditional love in her expectant face was all he needed to woo her.

When he approached the bed, Pressine tensed slightly.

"What is it?" Elinas dropped to one knee on the deep blue rug at the side of the bed and caressed the satiny skin of her bare arm. "Apprehensive?"

She offered a timid smile. "A little."

"Not afraid of me, are you?" Her cheek felt soft under the light brush of his fingers.

"No." The shake of her pretty head sent lustrous waves through her raven tresses. "Should I be?"

"I would never harm you. All I want is to see you happy and safe." Leaving her silver coronet in place, Elinas picked a flower from the wreath crowning her hair and caressed her cheeks with the petals. "Your immodest behavior at the high table this afternoon certainly stirred my lusty impulses."

Pressine blushed. Such innocence....

Elinas lifted the wreath of wild flowers from her head. "Ouch!"

He had pricked his finger on a hidden pin. Laughing, he sent the wreath sailing and brought the injured fingertip to his mouth.

* * *

Pressine laughed with him, her scalp tingling from his loving touch. Slowly, the mirth died between them. The gleam of the king's dark eyes spoke of feral depths. Would she enjoy the experience?

From listening to women talk, she gathered that a few delighted in the deed, but many loathed it. Suddenly, she wondered whether she could trust Elinas. He was but a man, and she knew nothing of the fierceness of a lover. Would he rend her apart, injuring her in his haste to satisfy his hunger?

"I need a skilled healer," Elinas murmured, holding his bloody thumb to her half-open lips.

Sustaining his piercing gaze, Pressine licked the warm, viscous blood tasting of rich copper. She derived a sensual pleasure from the intimate contact with his very life force, as if they sealed in blood a pact more binding than any wedding vow. When the finger grew insistent, demanding entry into her mouth, she felt inexplicably aroused by the impetuous intrusion. But when Elinas withdrew it, she missed the contact, feeling suddenly abandoned and wanting.

Disappointment must have shown on her face. Elinas eased her on the bed and embraced her, his face so close, she could hear his breath and feel the wind of it on her parted lips. Her heart beat faster as he hovered, blocking the candlelight with his wide frame, then gently covered her mouth with his. She closed her eyes.

This would never do. Driven by a sudden urge, Pressine opened her lips, inviting his imperious tongue to penetrate and invade her. The whirlwind of his kiss filled her mind and body. As if the world around her ceased to exist, she abandoned herself to the sensual pleasures of his lips and mouth. When the kiss ended in soft long strokes, she lay shaking and panting.

Elinas beamed, breathless, a look of wonder flooding his dark features. "I always suspected you would be a gifted lover despite your inexperience, my lady, but the blaze in your belly burns hotter than the fires of Bel. Are you already familiar with lovemaking?"

Pressine's heart leapt. Had she made a mistake? "Was I too forward, my lord? I know not what is expected of me... I followed an impulse."

"And a grand impulse at that!" His soft laugh held great tenderness. "Please do not hold back on my account."

"All right." Relieved, Pressine allowed her smile to return.

"Be as wild as your nature dictates, my love. I am not one to shy away from a spirited wife. On the contrary." The king nibbled her ear, his strong hand traveling from her waist up the curve of her round breasts.

Under his firm grip, Pressine found it difficult to breathe, like a doe pinned under a lion's paw. Elinas could certainly impose his whim on her by sheer physical force. While the thought frightened her a little, it thrilled her more.

Butterfly kisses flew from her throat down to the low neckline of the golden dress where the hardening orbs of her breasts swelled under his expert touch. His soft tongue caressed the hills and valleys of her chest, nestling in her cleavage, teasing at the edge of the golden fabric, searching to free her hard buds from the constraints of the dress.

Pressine combed small fingers through his thick black hair and cradled his head against her. The fragrance of marjoram in his stubby beard made her smile. An unusual refinement for a man. When Elinas dislodged a nipple and caught it gently between his teeth, she cried in surprise, arching under his strong hands.

Her body tensed, and her fingers tightened in his hair. Her breast hardened to the point of aching. Elinas nibbled and suckled on the sensitive tip, the sensation stirring wondrous desires in the warmth growing between her thighs. Cries escaped her in ragged breaths while her body undulated of its own volition, seeking contact.

Elinas retreated, leaving her wet breast exposed to the cool draft, then looked into her eyes with an intensity Pressine had never seen in a man. She shuddered at the thought of so much passion.

"I love you," he said hoarsely. "You are mine forever, and I shall never let anything come between us. I could not stand losing you... ever. I love you too much."

"And I love you, my lord," she replied, savoring the strange words that sounded so right.

The recollections of two nights ago, when she had tried to imagine what Elinas would feel like, rekindled her yearning for the contact of his skin. Her hand furrowed through the opening of his tunic, into his white linen shirt, to feel the hard muscles tightening on his broad, hairy chest. A male scent assailed her senses, making her nostrils flare like those of the mare in heat.

Elinas' large hand running up her leg crumpled the golden fabric of the gown. Heat suffused her thighs. Lost in a maelstrom of overwhelming sensations, as light kisses rained on her bare throat and shoulders, Pressine hardly noticed the deft fingers unlacing the ties of her dress. Soon, having stripped her to the thin chemise, Elinas half rose to pull shirt and tunic over his head.

Pressine admired the perfect line of his shoulders, the strong muscles of his arms. She could not help but compare him to Bodvar, the only other man she had seen naked. Where the dazed Viking had been hard and cold as stone, pale as death itself, and forbidding in his trembling delirium, her king's darker body looked deliciously warm, alive, caring and welcoming.

The trews came off.

"Mighty Goddess!" Her hand flew to her mouth as Pressine gasped at the sight of his erect manhood. It was huge. How could this thing possibly fit in her and not damage anything?

"I promise to be gentle," he said in a reassuring whisper, lowering himself beside her on the bed.

"Hold me tight," she pleaded, unsure whether she could stand the certain pain that must come, but determined to perform her duty to the man she loved and to the Goddess who ordered their union.

His hands caressed her thighs as he pulled up her thin chemise. Pressine trembled slightly, feeling exposed and vulnerable. She had not experience shyness while bathing nude at the spring. So why now?

"Bel be praised." Elinas stared at her as if she were a rare jewel. "I have missed this wondrous sight."

"So you did spy on me on that first day." She found the strength to tease him. "I always suspected it but never dared ask." That was a white lie. She had known all along.

His eyes fixed on her, he pressed his warm skin against hers. Pressine felt an immediate connection, as if she could read his mind. His yearning, his concern for her, his genuine love lay bare for her to see.

Relishing the insistent roaming of his hands, she closed her eyes and surrendered to his caress, losing herself in the pleasure of his demanding touch. Every inch of her body he fondled with fingers or tongue, exacting sighs and cries. When his head lowered to the junction of her thighs, however, Pressine stopped breathing and looked up in surprise to discover that she wanted him there. His expert tongue opened the delicate petals of her virginal flower, teasing, making her hunger for a stronger contact.

"Please," she whispered, not caring what kind of release she was asking for, knowing only that she wanted more than these delicious ministrations.

Her heart skipped a beat when she felt him move up. As he loomed above her and their eyes met, he stopped suddenly, as if unsure, a puzzled look on his face.

"Please," Pressine asked again, her breathing fast and short. "Make me yours, my lord. I am ready to feel the brunt of your passion."

"Yes! I can see it in your eyes." His face relaxed. With infinite tenderness, his arms encircled her in a tight embrace.

Trapped against his chest, lost in a turmoil of bewildering sensations, committed to let it happen, Pressine closed her eyes in surrender. She had a short intake at his insistent push against her secret gate, but she met him half way, opening up to receive him, her soft flesh yielding around the hardness of him. Nothing, however had prepared her for what followed.

She gasped, then cried. Deep into her very core something broke, releasing a hot viscous wave. Elinas paused, but she urged him on. The exquisite, intimate contact enhanced the glimpse of mind reading she had experienced at the feel of his warm skin. She could feel what he felt.

At her urging, Elinas rode her hard. Anticipating his need, Pressine moved with him, enjoying his delight as well as her own. Warm blissful sensations drowned the memory of discomfort. Pressine lost herself in the sweet smell of him, the contact of his drenched skin, the sheer weight of his body.

Under the power of his ramming thrust, the pleasure fed her ravenous hunger. She heard loud moans and cries, then realized they came from her very core. At last, she felt the tremors of his release flooding her.

She held him tight for a long time, eyes closed, not wanting to let him go. When she finally loosened her embrace, with a deep sigh and a smile, Elinas eased himself off to lie beside her.

Pressine kissed the tip of his shoulder. "I have never felt more complete and serene."

His mouth found her lips, and she responded wholeheartedly, arching under his caress.

When he let go of her, she could not stand the void. "How could I possibly sleep now? I still want you."

He emitted a soft laugh. "By the fires of Bel, woman, I shall gladly keep you company as long as it takes."

She pulled herself up on the skins covering the bed. "Would it be much of a bother to do it again?"

"Delighted to oblige, my lady." His hand played with a strand of her hair. "But this time, let us take our time about it and pleasure each other in different ways."

"You mean there is more to this wondrous act?"

His rich laugh resounded through the bedchamber. "Much more, believe me. And I shall not rest before I have taught you everything I know."

"Then we had better start," she whispered.

For a brief moment, in the back of her mind, a warning voice told her that Mattacks would never stop hounding her, the Vikings might return anytime, and she should, more than ever, beware of the curse...

But on this particular night, she pushed away the troubling thoughts. When Elinas nibbled her ear, Pressine immersed herself into a world of reeling sensations from which she never wanted to return. Duty and the Goddess could wait. For now she would forget the harsh world and enjoy this newfound happiness with the man she loved.

The End

Curse of the Lost Isle series
(medieval fantasy romance):

Princess of Bretagne – Book 1
Pagan Queen – Book 2
Seducing Sigefroi – Book 3
Lady of Luxembourg – Book 4
Chatelaine of Forez -- Book 5
Special Edition (First three books)

Ancient Enemy series (sci-fi romance):
Anaz-voohri – Book One
Relics – Book Two
Kicking Bots – Book Three

Archangel books (speculative fiction):
Crusader – Book One
Checkmate – Book Two

Ashes for the Elephant God (reincarnation love story)

Snatched (Sci-fi Romance)

Alien Lockdown (Sci-fi Romance)

Chat with Vijaya and other Books We Love authors in
the Books We Love Online Book Club:
https://www.facebook.com/groups/153824114796417/

About the Author

Born in France, award-winning author Vijaya Schartz never conformed to anything and could never refuse a challenge. She likes action and exotic settings, in life and on the page. She traveled the world and claims she also travels through time as she writes the past and the future with the same ease. Her books collected many five star reviews and literary awards. She makes you believe you actually lived these extraordinary adventures among her characters. Her stories have been compared to Indiana Jones with sizzling romance. So, go ahead, dare to experience the magic, and she will keep you entranced, turning the pages until the last line.

Find more about her and her books on her website at
http://www.vijayaschartz.com

http://bookswelove.net

If you're looking for something spicier, visit:
http://spicewelove.com